Between Us Girls

Also by Joe Orton

Autobiography
The Orton Diaries

Novels
Head to Toe
The Boy Hairdresser *and* Lord Cucumber

Plays
The Visitors *and* Fred and Madge
The Complete Plays

Screenplay
Up Against It

Between Us Girls

a novel by

JOE ORTON

INTRODUCTION
BY FRANCESCA COPPA

GROVE PRESS
New York

Published simultaneously in Canada
Printed in the United States of America

FIRST GROVE PRESS EDITION

Library of Congress Cataloging-in-Publication Data

Orton, Joe.
    Between us girls : a novel / by Joe Orton ;
introduction by
  Francesca Coppa.
      p.   cm.
     ISBN 0-8021-3644-3
     I. Title.
    PR6065.R7B48   1999
    823'.914—dc21   99-19630
                                       CIP

Grove Press
841 Broadway
New York, NY 10003

99 00 01 02 10 9 8 7 6 5 4 3 2 1

Introduction

In 1963, an unknown writer named John Kingsley Orton submitted a radio play to the BBC. It was accepted, subject to revision. During the short time between the play's acceptance and its broadcast, Orton not only revised his play but recreated himself. John Kingsley Orton's last work, *The Boy Hairdresser*, became Joe Orton's first work, *The Ruffian on the Stair*.

The name change from John Kingsley to Joe was not purely superficial. Having attracted the attention of both the theatrical establishment and the greater public, the newly christened 'Joe' carefully crafted a personality and a history to go with his new name. Asked for an autobiographical sketch for the programme of *Entertaining Mr Sloane*, Orton wrote:

> I was born in Leicester. I didn't get the 11 plus. I went to what, I suppose, is now called a secondary modern school. I've been married. And divorced. I've worked at various jobs, including unloading chocolates at Cadbury's railway sidings, helping in the making of sex hormones at the British Drug Houses and cleaning the lenses on spectacles. I was in prison for six months in 1962 for larceny (not really as grand as it seems.) This is my first full-length play, though I wrote one before this which the BBC have bought. Nobody knows when it's to be put on . . . Oh, I'm thirty-one. Since I came out of prison in September 1962 I've been living on the National Assistance.
> Is that enough?

The version of himself that Orton promoted was calculated to emphasise the authenticity of his working-class background and the rawness of his talent. To further support this image of Joe Orton, novice writer, Orton shrewdly lowered his age from thirty-one to twenty-five in the final version of his programme biography.

The press fell in love with the idea of the 25-year-old, working-class, novice playwright, and thrust him into the national spotlight. They turned the young, attractive and photogenic Orton into a poster boy for the new British theatre, and his image – the playwright in T-shirt and leather jacket, arms crossed, pouting into the camera against the background of a seedy North London street – accompanied articles with headlines like 'Theatre's New Star Signs on the Dole,' 'What Prison Did for this Playwright,' and 'It's Still Fish and Chips for Joe Orton.' At the centre of these articles were what one newspaper wit quickly catalogued as the five *clichés* of the Orton story – his prison record (*cliché* No. 1), working-class background (*cliché* No. 2), failure to pass the 11 plus (*cliché* No. 3), time on the National Assistance (*cliché* No. 4) and tough public image, complete with chic leather jacket (*cliché* No. 5).

While all of these clichés were in fact true – Orton had been to prison, was genuinely working class, etc. – they also served to distract attention from the fact that he was far from a novice talent. By 1964, Orton had been a serious, if unsuccessful, writer for over ten years, and had written at least eight novels and three plays, some alone, and others in collaboration with his lover and partner Kenneth Halliwell. Orton claimed that *Entertaining Mr Sloane* was his first full-length play, but it was actually his first full-length work *to reach the public*, a distinction he rarely chose to emphasise.

However, the more astute of Orton's early critics realised almost from the beginning that there was something fishy about Orton's public self-presentation. *Entertaining Mr Sloane* seemed too sophisticated to have been the first play of the 25-year-old tough currently being showcased in the newspapers. Milton Shulman noted in the *Evening Standard* that 'Joe Orton, who is said to be 25 years old, is either a true primitive, or a subtle sophisticate, or he is three playwrights masquerading as one.' Similarly, Harold Hobson observed in *The Sunday Times* that he would not call the new playwright's first play 'promising,' as it seemed to him 'more of an end than a beginning.'

Entertaining Mr Sloane was more of an end than a beginning: it was the final product of a literary process which had begun ten years earlier. Joe Orton actually began writing in 1953, a full ten years before he became successful as a playwright. His career can, in fact, be divided into three distinct phases, and the canonical Orton works are products of the third phase, representing only part of Orton's total literary output. In the earliest part of his career, 1953 to 1956, Orton wrote as a junior partner in collaboration with Halliwell. Together they produced at least five novels, including *The Silver Bucket* (1953), *Lord Cucumber* (1954), *The Mechanical Womb* (1955), *The Last Days of Sodom* (1955), and the first of three works to be entitled *The Boy Hairdresser* (1956). While these novels attracted the attention of various publishers, they were all ultimately rejected. In the latter part of 1956, Orton and Halliwell decided to sever their literary partnership (although they would reunite once, in 1960, to produce the second work called *The Boy Hairdresser*). From 1956 to 1962, John Orton wrote as an independent author, producing two novels, *Between Us Girls* (1957) and *The Vision of Gombold Proval* (1961; published in 1971 as *Head to Toe*), and two plays: *Fred and*

Madge (1959) and *The Visitors* (1961). Orton's third play, *The Ruffian on the Stair*, marks the beginning of his mature career, a career cut tragically short when Halliwell murdered Orton, then killed himself in August 1967.

Joe Orton's mature works – seven plays, a risqué (and rejected) screenplay for the Beatles, and a literary diary unique in its combination of wit and sexual frankness – have had an enormous impact both on drama and on the culture at large. The plays have earned him a central place among twentieth-century dramatists, and Orton's diary, which covers the last nine months of his life, is famous as a comic literary masterpiece, as a gay history, and as a socio-cultural record, as it chronicles Orton's vision of himself as a writer, as a homosexual man, and as a part of so-called 'Swinging London' during the so-called 'Summer of Love'. Furthermore, Orton's combination of subversive wit and pro-gay sensibility in the years before gay was good has earned him a kind of sainthood comparable to Oscar Wilde's among those interested in reconstructing gay culture and history. Most tellingly, the adjective 'Ortonesque' has firmly entered the lexicon as a precise way of describing a certain kind of provocative and outrageous comic vision.

Thirty years after his death, the publication of Joe Orton's surviving early works – *Lord Cucumber*, *Between Us Girls*, *Fred and Madge*, *The Boy Hairdresser*, and *The Visitors* – allows us to trace the development of Orton's extraordinary talent. Born to a working-class family in Leicester in 1933, John Kingsley Orton was an unlikely heir to Wilde, Austen and Congreve: he was a literary foundling if ever there was one. And yet, even Orton's very earliest writings – the juvenile diaries he kept between 1949 and 1951, between the ages of 16 and 18 – illustrate a determination, or even desperation, to make something of himself despite a lack of resources, encouragement, or support. It was this determination which kept Orton writing through ten long years of failure, slowly developing the literary themes, techniques and style that would one day make him famous.

While Orton's adolescent diaries confirm his teachers' dismissive assessments of him – that he was semi-literate, that he couldn't spell – they also show his earliest attempts to self-educate and self-improve. Theatre was always Orton's chosen escape route. He joined a number of amateur dramatic societies, and his diaries record his desire to get parts, to improve his speaking voice, and to increase his grace and poise.

> 4 April 1949: Bought book its called *Look Your Best*. I wanted (for some hitherto undiscovered and probaly sentimental reason) *Richard III*, but couldn't get it. Found myself unconsciously think what I would say when asked to take part in a broadcast called 'How I became an actor' probably start, 'I think I have always had a sort of yearning etc etc' Pull myself together quickly.

Sixteen-year-old John Kingsley Orton saves money to buy books, theatre albums, and elocution lessons. Brought up in an anti-intellectual family and community, Orton nevertheless became a voracious reader, getting 'lots of books out of the Library' and using them to fill his many 'quiet' – which Orton always mis-spelt 'quite' – days. Orton's juvenile diaries also show him to be striving for personal and literary sophistication, and for wit:

> 24 February 1949: Our photos came today they are very good. Mam took them work the forewoman said she didn't know where we got our looks

from as we didn't get it from mam. (Query: to believe or not to be, lieve.)

But Orton's quest for self-improvement was occurring in the vacuum of Leicester, and he was without the support of friends or family. It was none other than Laurence Olivier, via a newspaper article, who gave Orton hope that he might be able to attend RADA, the Royal Academy of Dramatic Art in London:

15 April 1950: Have been reading an article about the stage by Laurence Olivier. He says that there are scholarships one can win to the RADA. And for the exceptionally talented there are maintenance grants as well. Hope one of those elocution teachers I wrote to answers my letter. I should think one of them will. Failing this, I'll write to RADA itself. I know this address is GOWER ST., LONDON. But I must get an evenings job and how.

A line runs down the page from the word 'scholarships' to a plaintive note at the bottom – 'get it please'. Orton's desperation was fuelled by his hatred of the boring routines of menial work: his juvenile diary is a litany of complaints.

24 January 1949: Work, how I hate it in the morning when Dad says 'its 10 to seven' . . .

27 January 1949: Not a very good day. Finished all my work so asked Horace he gave me some work. I didn't like cleaning ink wells.

21 April 1949: Mr Yates didn't come to work today so I had to help Becky (Miss Henry in Post room it was dead awful.)

But Orton's attempts to achieve something better were scoffed at by those around him: 'He came to me one day and said "I'm very interested in the theatre and the only thing I want to do is go on the stage",' remembered one of his teachers. 'I dismissed it.' But Orton stubbornly clung to his aspirations, seizing every opportunity to better himself and fighting tenaciously for small acting roles in local productions. On 17 June 1950, Orton recorded in his diary that he 'pulled an old dresser to pieces am trying to make a bookcase out of it if I can but there doesn't seem to be much good wood in it.' The future writer's rather poignant attempt to build a bookcase, in his world an uncommon and generally unnecessary piece of furniture, out of the meagre scrap materials then available to him is symptomatic of the frustrations Orton faced in his struggle to become an artist and an intellectual, to become the kind of person who would want a bookcase in the first place.

Orton continued to work at jobs he hated in order to pay for elocution lessons: he wanted to improve the quality of his voice, and dampen the strong vowel sounds of his Leicester accent. The coaching apparently helped; Orton was accepted at RADA against considerable odds, and left Leicester for London in 1951. A month after the term started he stopped writing his juvenile diary, though not before he recorded having met Kenneth Halliwell, who was also enrolled in the acting classes. Once famous as a playwright, Orton tended to downplay his desire for an acting career. When his theatrical training later came up in press interviews, Orton tended to talk about his three-month postgraduate stint as an assistant stage-manager, emphasising its similarity to menial labour, and not about his histrionic ability or aspirations, or his love of the theatre as an adolescent. Acting, however, was Orton's primary focus in the late forties and early fifties – as indeed it was Halliwell's – and only after their acting careers fizzled out did they begin their productive literary partnership.

Kenneth Halliwell, Orton's partner and lover, was initially the more accomplished writer. Halliwell's first work, a play called *The Protagonist*, dates from 1949, and was written for the Carlton Players, the local dramatic society in Halliwell's home town of Bebington, a suburb of Liverpool. Written before Halliwell went to RADA, the play is in many ways immature; however, it provides suggestive clues about the character of its twenty-three-year-old author. The play dramatises the life of the actor Edmund Kean, but Halliwell shapes the story so as to emphasise and celebrate Kean's social and sexual defiance.

Underneath *The Protagonist's* surface level of biographical melodrama is a homosexual conflict disguised as a heterosexual one. Halliwell has Kean confront a threat that would have been very real to him as an active homosexual in Britain in the late 1940s: the choice of blackmail or ruin as a result of overstepping the bounds of socially acceptable sexual behaviour. Halliwell's Kean has an affair with a treacherous married woman, who turns his love letters over to her blackmailer husband. Faced with the threat of a lawsuit and public exposure of his adultery unless he pays, the iconoclastic Kean refuses to settle. 'Though I be legally forced to pay, yet I'll drag that strumpet through the courts. All England shall see where the right lies. Though the strict law may go against me.' Society cannot tolerate such honesty, and the great Edmund Kean is destroyed. But by having his protagonist refuse sexual shame and proudly proclaim what conventional morality demands he deny, Halliwell makes Kean into an early martyr of the sexual revolution in general and of gay liberation in particular; Halliwell's Kean 'comes out' as a sexual nonconformist, and his passionate arguments in favour of sexual freedom – codified and condensed – would be on pro-gay banners, buttons and bumper-stickers by the late sixties. Edmund Kean was Kenneth Halliwell's idea of a hero, and his creation in 1949 shows that Halliwell was socially, if not artistically, *avant-garde*.

The Protagonist thus gives us a rare, if sketchy, view of the young Kenneth Halliwell; it indicates that Halliwell was a romantic, that he was educated, that he endorsed moral and sexual defiance, and that he was ambitious. One can imagine how these qualities impressed John Kingsley Orton, who had only recently – and with great difficulty – escaped a life of harshness, deprivation and restriction. Up until recently, Orton had felt tethered to an abusive home and a menial job, and Halliwell, whose pose and prose were expansive, overblown, larger-than-life, must have staggered him. In light of the pathos of Halliwell's last years, it may be difficult to imagine him as a Byronic hero; yet that was certainly how he must have appeared to Orton in 1951. When Kenneth Halliwell abandoned acting for writing, John Kingsley Orton signed on as his apprentice. As the senior writer of the team, Halliwell dominated their early works; however, he also unselfishly and effectively nurtured Orton's talent.

Kenneth Halliwell was an ideal mentor for Orton because he possessed, as John Lahr aptly noted in *Prick Up Your Ears*, vocabulary, tenacity, and a sense of literary tradition. Halliwell, who was well and widely educated, was deeply interested in what, for lack of better words, we now might call the queer literary canon; he had identified a strain within the broader literary tradition with which he particularly identified, and to which he wished to contribute as a writer. Halliwell schooled Orton in these works, from the ancient Greeks to Christopher Marlowe to Jean Genet, and Orton came to share his literary tastes and perspective. Together they attempted to write works with a distinctively homosexual sensibility, and their early novels are all profoundly influenced by the style of Halliwell's literary idol, Ronald Firbank.

Firbank is the real godfather of contemporary gay literature, since he was the first author in the modern era to write queerly with a clear view of the potential consequences. Firbank was nine at the time of Wilde's trials in 1895, and they obsessed him throughout his life: he clearly understood the risks and ramifications of his own militant homosexuality. Nevertheless, Firbank was the first author to pick up the threads of aestheticism that had been dropped by Oscar Wilde, deliberately connecting himself to literature which was widely regarded as tainted, or even poisonous. In *Prancing Novelist: a Defence of Fiction in the Form of a Critical Biography of Ronald Firbank*, Brigid Brophy notes that:

> Just as he put into modern practice Oscar Wilde's aesthetic theory, so Firbank modernised Oscar Wilde's camp. Firbank is perhaps the inventor, certainly the fixer, of modern camp. Popes, cardinals, choirboys, nuns, flagellants, queens (both senses): all the classic camp dramatis personae are his. He borrowed even Wilde's engaging camp habit of sending up the Queen (regnant sense). Their queen – Wilde's and the one set firm in the imagination of Firbank, who was 15 when she died – was of course Queen Victoria.

'Sign your name Queen Victoria,' cajoles Inspector Truscott in Orton's *Loot*, 'no one would tamper with her account.' Firbank's classic camp cast of characters, sassed up for the sixties, reappear in Joe Orton's mature plays; in his adult diary, Orton refers to Firbank respectfully as 'the source'. It was Kenneth Halliwell who gave Orton his taste for Firbank, who outlined and then radicalised Orton's literary tradition. Firbank deeply admired Wilde, who had admired Jane Austen; Orton, trained by the Firbank-influenced Halliwell, was later pegged 'the Oscar Wilde of Welfare State Gentility', and was delighted when he was compared to Austen. It was the astute *Sunday Times* critic Harold Hobson who made the connection:

> I hope I shall not be misunderstood if I say that the English author of whom Joe Orton in *Entertaining Mr Sloane* reminds me most vividly is Jane Austen. Miss Austen had a keen eye for the absurdities of the fashionable fiction of her day; and so has Mr Orton. His *Entertaining Mr Sloane*, all proportions kept, is the *Northanger Abbey* of our contemporary stage.

'Hobson was the only critic who spotted what Sloane was,' Orton later admitted. 'This was absolutely amazing. I wrote him a letter saying that I've always admired Austen's juvenilia.'

Even after Orton became successful, Halliwell continued to encourage his development, pushing him to broaden the scope of his works, to expand his literary boundaries, to extend his frame of reference. In his diary, Orton records how Halliwell directed his literary career:

> I had the idea that the play I intend to write set in prison, *Where Love Lies Bleeding*, should be, in the main, a satire on Genet using much of the story of *Querelle of Brest*. K.H. said, 'You must use all Genet's subjects – beautiful young murderers, buggery, treachery, bent and brutal policemen and theft.

And it was Halliwell, the former classics scholar, who pushed Orton to connect his work back to the ancient Greeks, the starting point of any gay male tradition. As Orton noted in his diary:

> I've finished typing *What the Butler Saw* today. Yesterday Kenneth read the script and was enthusiastic – he made several important suggestions which I'm carrying out. He was impressed by the way in which, using the context of a farce, I'd managed to produce a *Golden Bough* subtext – even (he pointed out) the castration of Sir Winston Churchill (the father-figure) and the descent of the god at the end – Sergeant Match, drugged and dressed in a woman's gown. It was only to be expected that Kenneth would get these references to classical literature. Whether anyone else will spot them is another matter. 'You must get a director who, while making it funny, brings out the subtext,' Kenneth said. He suggests that the dress Match wears should be of something suggestive of leopard skin – this would make it funny when Nick wears it and get the right 'image' for the Euripidean ending when Match wears it.

On the surface, Orton is praising Halliwell for 'recognising' his classical literary allusions; however, the parenthetical '(he pointed out)' shows Orton admitting that something more complex was happening. The passage – which is quite different from Orton's normal way of discussing his writing – has the tone of a student quickly reviewing notes given by an admired teacher. Kenneth Halliwell was not simply 'getting' Orton's themes, but discovering them, or even creating them, and by doing so, helping to knit Orton into the greater literary tradition.

Halliwell and Orton's early novels – *The Silver Bucket, Lord Cucumber, The Mechanical Womb, The Last*

Days of Sodom, and the first version of *The Boy Hair-dresser* – were all rejected by publishers, largely, if you read between the lines, on the grounds that they were too queer for mainstream audiences. In the days before the power of the pink pound was recognised, publishers thought that the homosexual audience was too small and too marginalised to be addressed. However, the importance of these works in the development of the Orton style was critical. Imitating Firbank gave Orton not only a tone, but a methodology he would use throughout his career: collage.

Ronald Firbank was a literary mosaicist who wrote phrases on bits of paper which he eventually synthesised into a final product. Orton adopted a similar technique; he composed pages and pages of discrete phrases and fragments which he only later grouped into sentences, paragraphs, and pages. Orton wrote a novel's worth of words, just not in any particular order; compiling pages of unusual adjectives (affably, athletically, allergically, apocalyptically), prospective titles (*Under Mummy, Leave Her Alone, Phallic Necessity, Up the Nape, Hips and Whores, Queer Cactus, Emerald Has Been Stung by a Wasp*), and impressionistic Firbankian sentences:

> The sea was grey, marbled with glittering crests.
> Brown and silver gardens came down to the pink
> water.
> Pendant globes of orange and blue striped fruit.
> A picture of a gold woman with crimson eyes,
> wrapped in fur.
> Windows like three orange eyes peering out of
> the fog.
> A sea like luminous milk.

Orton composed page after page of sentences like these, crossing them out as he placed them within a work. He continued to use this collage technique after he became a successful playwright; then, however, he compiled massive lists of more developed, distinctly 'Ortonesque' phrases which could be inserted into a play as necessary. These lists contain lines from Orton's major plays which, conceived out of context, now seem intrinsic to the plays in which they were used; they also provide us with a glimpse at the plays Orton might later have written:

- I doubt whether anything about a man's private parts would interest her. She treats them like bound volumes of Dickens. Peeping now and then when some musical tells her they're the 'in' thing.

- Are you a good boy?
- Yes.
- Why are you wasting my time then?

- Anyone over forty is led to believe that the younger generation are sexually insatiable. Isn't this true?
- No, sir.
- Another cherished belief exploded. The iconoclasm of today's youth is terrifying.

Orton also left us a list of appropriately 'Ortonesque' titles for these unwritten works. Orton used two of them – *Until She Screams* and *Up Against It* – before he died. We can only imagine the plays that would have been appended to some of the others: *Men and Boys*; *The Four-Letter Word Revue*; *Gwen, Maddened by Lust*; *By the Short Hairs*. One such title, suggested by Halliwell, was intended for Orton's next play, which was to be set at the coronation of Edward VII. Instead, John Lahr used it to title Orton's biography: *Prick Up Your Ears*.

After co-authoring their five failed Firbankian novels, Orton and Halliwell stopped collaborating. In a 1957 letter, Orton informed the publisher Charles Monteith of Faber and Faber that 'Kenneth and I have decided that there is very little to be gained by our collaboration and so we have split (for the purpose of writing).' By this time, Orton had already learned enough from Halliwell (and Firbank) to consider going out on his own; he had absorbed a literary tradition, adopted a non-naturalistic style, and developed a writing process which suited him. He had also mastered many of Halliwell's accomplishments: now Orton also had vocabulary, tenacity and a literary tradition. By fully utilising his two resources – Kenneth Halliwell and the public library – the determined Orton, like many autodidacts, had given himself a better education than most of the more fortunate get in school. Halliwell had shared his knowledge and skills with Orton, but it was Orton himself who was able to parlay those assets into a successful literary career.

No one can say with specificity or scientific precision why one writer fails while another succeeds. However, Orton's early solo work shows that he had one definite advantage over Kenneth Halliwell: he was interested in and paying attention to trends in contemporary writing. Orton and Halliwell began to write separately at some time in late 1956, a year which has come to be regarded as a watershed in British cultural history. Few contemporary British histories fail to note that 1956 was the year of John Osborne's *Look Back in Anger*, a play that was said to have triggered a dramatic revolution. Osborne and his semi-autobiographical protagonist, Jimmy Porter, were quickly described as 'angry young men', a label that connected them to fiction writers such as Kingsley Amis and John Wain, and to the young pop philosopher Colin Wilson, whose best-selling book *The Outsider* was published in the same month that

Look Back in Anger premiered. Although these writers denied that they formed any sort of cohesive literary movement, the artistic press found the idea hard to resist, and hyped both 'angry literature' and 'the new drama', helping to create a market for both. As a result, novels featuring angry anti-heroes became popular in the late fifties, and a host of new playwrights, as diverse as Arnold Wesker, Robert Bolt, N.F. Simpson and Harold Pinter, energised the theatre.

While Kenneth Halliwell continued to write in the style of Firbank, producing *Priapus in the Shrubbery* in 1959, John Orton experimented with the popular new styles and forms. In the second, more independent phase of his career, Orton wrote a diary novel (*Between Us Girls*), an 'angry' novel (*The Boy Hairdresser*), a Swiftian satiric fable (*The Vision of Gombold Proval*), and two startlingly different plays: *Fred and Madge* and *The Visitors*. These works are striking in their diversity, and show Orton's desire to stretch himself, to learn to connect with an audience.

Between Us Girls was a crucial step for Orton; it was his first attempt to develop a literary voice distinct from Halliwell's. The very title of the novel announces a shift from the tone of the collaborative works. The classical archness of *The Last Days of Sodom* or *The Mechanical Womb* has been replaced by an earthier, warmer, more personal camp. The title *Between Us Girls* attempts to establish an intimacy with the reader, an intimacy Orton enhances by writing in the first person. The novel begins with protagonist Susan Hope's bubbly declaration 'I think I'm going crazy!' – a burst of colloquial speech that stands in striking contrast to the elaborate and witty syntactical wryness which characterises Halliwell's work. Orton's exploration of first person narrative in *Between Us Girls* illustrates his interest in the varieties, vagaries and vulgarities of speech, providing tantalising hints of the dramatist buried within the novelist.

In *Between Us Girls* Orton begins to sketch out the characters and themes that define his mature plays. Right off the bat, Orton's solo work illustrates one of the central characteristics of what would one day be called the Ortonesque: a disjunction between the realities of his characters' lives and the language they choose to describe those realities; in other words, a radical contrast between the events of the plot and the tone of the dialogue. *Between Us Girls* chronicles the adventures of Susan Hope,[1] aspiring starlet. The humour of the story lies in the fact that Susan lives in a fantasy world created by romantic fiction and the movies, and refuses to recognise the corruption of the real world in which she lives, and which hovers just behind the optimism of her rather pretentious prose:

> Sheila Gribble had a record of *Suddenly It's Moonlight*, the hit song from the new musical. Told Sheila it was just the thing I'd been looking for. Intend to sing it at my audition for the Rainier Revuebar.
> Sheila said: 'The Rainier Revuebar?'
> I said: 'Didn't you know? I had a letter from them the other day. I don't mind telling you I'm thrilled to death about it.'
> Sheila said: 'Daaarling. The Rainier Revuebar.'
> I said: 'It's a great chance for me if I get a job, only I'm worried about my lack of experience.'
> Sheila said: 'Daaarling! Experience? What kind of acting do you think they want on the new mirrored stage? Lady Macbeth?'
> Sheila Gribble is just a cat. I certainly shan't let myself be taken to any more of her parties.

The 'shan't' says everything about Susan. She is more concerned about her grammar than about the fact that she's auditioning for a sex show, and uses the mock-gentility of her language to decorate and disguise the more sordid aspects of her situation. In this way she prefigures the character of Kath in Orton's *Entertaining Mr Sloane* six years later:

KATH (*to* SLOANE): How could you behave so bad. Accusing me of seducing you.
SLOANE: But you did!
KATH: That's neither here nor there. Using expressions like that. Making yourself cheap.

Susan Hope is the first of Orton's characters to be obsessed with keeping up appearances and constructing a fatuous propriety which blocks out reality. Such is Susan Hope's level of denial that only a girlfriend's recollection of the plot of a film she once saw makes her realise that she hasn't been taken to Mexico to perform in a nightclub, as she has convinced herself:

'This film I saw once – it reminds me of that,' said Joan Fannyjohnson, breaking into a rare burst of speech . . .
'It's like a dream, isn't it? What was the film about, Joan?'
Joan stood up, looked toward the gates, gazed up at the walls and said: 'About the white slave trade.'
We sat quite still each one thinking her own thoughts. The doves cooed. The breeze ruffled the water. And I remembered – so many little things.

The owner of the white slave establishment is coyly named Liz Monteith, after Orton's friend, the publisher Charles Monteith; Orton was clearly sending Monteith a message by drawing a pointed analogy between publishers and pimps.

While Orton's artistic aspirations would continue to be frustrated for some years, in *Between Us Girls* Orton allows Susan Hope to attain hers. Like the characters in *The Importance of Being Earnest*, who find that their lives conform to the fictions they create about themselves, Susan Hope in fact manages to escape to Hollywood and the superstardom of which she dreams. On the first page of *Between Us Girls*, Susan excitedly buys the latest best-selling potboiler, *The Divine Marquisé*, and longs for her life to be like romantic, Mills and Boon-style fiction: 'I'd give seven years of my life to be swept off my feet by a handsome stranger – like Pompadour in *The Divine Marquisé*.' By the end of the novel, Susan Hope, now a star, is cast as Pompadour in the film to be made from the book. In a plot twist stolen straight out of the movie musical *Singin' in the Rain* (1952), the historical romance is turned into a musical, and Susan Hope gets to make the suggestion that the actor Donald O'Connor makes in the original film which results in *Singin' in the Rain*'s 'Broadway Melody' number: 'Can't Pompadour dream she's a twentieth-century chorus girl?'[2] Orton's Hollywood is based on Hollywood's 1952 version of 1920s Hollywood, and later, defending himself on charges of imitating Harold Pinter, Orton admitted the influence of American film on his work: 'I think there are other influences on my work far more important than Pinter, and of course you always have to remember that the things that influenced Pinter, which I believe are Hollywood movies in the forties, also influenced me.' In *Between Us Girls*, Orton trades Halliwell's elite queer classicism for the more popular and conventional camp of the American musical.

However, buried within *Between Us Girls* is the starting point of a crucial strand of John Kingsley Orton's literary development, and this strand begins with the character called Bob Kennedy. Kennedy marks the first appearance in any Orton work of what might reasonably be termed a hooligan or an 'angry young man', and his appearance in this novel is the most decisive mark of difference between Orton's work and Halliwell's. While Kenneth Halliwell was indisputably better educated than Orton, his literary imagination was fixated on the past. In contrast, *Between Us Girls* illustrates that Orton was open to and prepared to be influenced by *contemporary* culture in all its forms, whether it be the movies, the mood of his London, or the spate of 'angry young man' novels which were popular at the time he was writing. Bob Kennedy is the first Orton character to be firmly rooted in the fifties.

When Kennedy is first introduced into *Between Us Girls* he is drunk, and has a black eye. He is surly, pouting, and sexually ambiguous – a typical man-child of the fifties such as Brando or James Dean would play on film: 'He peeled the cigarette stump he was smoking away from his lip and ground it into an ashtray. Behind the baby face, far down, there lay a deep nihilism.' Bob Kennedy is almost out of place in *Between Us Girls* – it is practically impossible to imagine him coexisting in the same universe as Susan Hope, let alone marrying her, as he does at the story's conclusion. Toward the middle of the novel he walks Susan Hope home from a party:

> As we passed a large expanse of brick wall he
> stopped, felt in his pocket, and produced a piece
> of chalk. He ordered me to keep a look-out for
> anyone who might be walking that way. I went,
> as ordered, to the other side of the road while he
> wrote 'Go Home Yanks' and 'Ban Atom Bases'
> on the wall. We walked on again until he saw
> another wall upon which he wrote an indecent
> rhyme beginning, 'Is it true what they say about

Eton?' He was so exhausted by the effort of this that for a long while he couldn't speak. Finally he said: 'Don't you get sick of it?'

'Of what?'

'The Stage,' he said, eyeing me with ill-concealed contempt.

'No.'

This must have disgusted him more than he showed for when we reached my house he paused before ascending the steps to write on the wall: 'Hang the bleedin' actors.' I snatched his chalk and began to obliterate what he'd written. There was a scuffle, during which I threw the chalk over the fence into the next-door flowerbeds. Bob Kennedy swore, loudly and violently, kicked me on the ankle, and without even bothering to say goodnight, he walked away down the road.

'Go Home Yanks' and 'Ban Atom Bases' – these inscriptions (and the sentiments behind them) are as foreign to Susan Hope and her circle as Egyptian hieroglyphs. And yet, when she re-encounters Kennedy as a sailor on the ship that is taking her to Mexico, she (and the novel) becomes sexually fixated on him:

> The sun had turned his face to burnt-gold. He looked terribly handsome: sex personified. I felt a tremendous physical attraction to him. The impact was like a blow. The blood rushed to my cheeks.
>
> He looked at me, and a slow smile formed on his lips. 'What are you doing here?' he said. His eyes burned.
>
> I could feel my blood-pressure rising. My God, Susan, I told myself, 'what's happening to you?'

Later, Kennedy is captured by the white slavers while trying to rescue Susan, and Orton happily has Bob

Kennedy prostituted with the rest of the 'girls', costumed in 'a white sailor-suit several sizes too small with a lost look I told myself it would be easy to love.' Kennedy eventually engineers Susan's escape from the brothel, and delivers her to L.A. and movie stardom.

In a sense, one could argue that Kennedy was also responsible for John Kingsley Orton's escape and his future stardom as a playwright, for Bob Kennedy in his white sailor suit is the first of the young, beautiful, and bisexual hooligans who would populate Joe Orton's mature works. Orton recycled the Bob Kennedy scenes (and only those scenes) for his 1960 novel *The Boy Hairdresser* (the second work to bear that name, and his last attempt at collaboration with Kenneth Halliwell). Kennedy evolves into Donelly, the novel's protagonist. When Orton loosely reworked the novel of *The Boy Hairdresser* into the 1963 play of the same name, the play which became *The Ruffian on the Stair*, traces of Kennedy survive in Wilson, the play's titular ruffian. And he continues to resurface in the major Orton works: as the sex-object Sloane in *Entertaining Mr Sloane*, as the socially-resistant Ray in *The Good and Faithful Servant*, as the criminals Hal and Dennis in *Loot*, as the streetwise Caulfield in *Funeral Games*, and as the blackmailing gigolo Nick in *What the Butler Saw*. Orton succeeded as a playwright by marrying Halliwell's sense of classical literary construction and themes to characters and situations that were distinctively and decisively of their moment.

In fact, with his creation of Bob Kennedy in *Between Us Girls*, John Kingsley Orton took the first step toward his own eventual transformation into Joe Orton – the successful playwright as swaggering hooligan, ex-convict, working-class tough in a leather jacket. John Kingsley Orton, student of Kenneth Halliwell, RADA-trained actor, writer of ten years' experience and vast determination, became the novice writer Joe Orton, a character who, like Kennedy himself, was perfectly expressive of the spirit and desires of his time.

FRANCESCA COPPA

Notes

1 The Hope girls are minor characters mentioned in Ronald Firbank's only play *The Princess Zoubaroff*. (One character notes: 'I consider the eldest Miss Hope a disgrace to England!')

2 The Assistant Director of the film of *The Divine Marquisé* is archly named 'O'Connor'; in *The Celluloid Closet*, Vito Russo notes that a line of dialogue between Donald O'Connor and Gene Kelly in *Singin' in the Rain* was pencilled out 'because it gave a hint of sexual perversion' between the two men, whose characters are longtime friends and show-business partners:

When O'Connor gets the idea of dubbing the voice of Debbie Reynolds for the high-pitched, tinny vice of Jean Hagen in a proposed musical, The Dancing Cavalier, he illustrates his idea for Kelly by standing in front of Reynolds and mouthing the words to 'Good Morning' while she sings behind him. When the song is over, O'Connor turns to Kelly and asks, 'Well? Convincing?' Kelly, not yet catching on, takes it as a joke and replies, 'Enchanting! What are you doing later?' The joke was eliminated. (Vito Russo, *The Celluloid Closet*. New York: Harper and Row, 1987, p. 99)

It is O'Connor, the asexual 'third wheel' of the trio of *Singin' in the Rain's* stars whose name is cited in *Between Us Girls*: perhaps Orton sensed that the scene cited above, with O'Connor standing in for Reynolds, provided a moment of emotional truth in the film.

Joe Orton: a Chronology

1933	*1 January:* John Kingsley Orton born in Leicester
1944	Orton fails his eleven-plus exam
1945-47	Orton attends Clark's College
1949	Orton begins writing his juvenile diary
1950	*April:* Orton takes elocution lessons
	November: Orton applies to the Royal Academy of Dramatic Art (RADA) in London
1951	*May:* Orton starts at RADA
	June: Orton moves in with Kenneth Halliwell at 161 West End Lane, London
	June: Orton stops writing juvenile diary
1953	*April:* Orton and Halliwell graduate from RADA
	April–July: Orton works as assistant stage manager at Ipswich Rep in Suffolk
	Halliwell and Orton begin collaborating on novels
	Halliwell and Orton write *The Silver Bucket* (novel, now lost)
1954	Halliwell and Orton write *Lord Cucumber* (novel)
1955	Halliwell and Orton write *The Mechanical Womb* (novel, now lost)
	Halliwell and Orton write *The Last Days of Sodom* (novel, now lost)
1956	Halliwell and Orton write *The Boy Hairdresser* (a novel in verse, now lost)
1957	*June:* Orton announces in a letter to the publisher Charles Monteith that he and

Kenneth Halliwell have begun to write separately

Orton writes *Between Us Girls* (novel)

1959 Orton and Halliwell move to 25 Noel Road, Islington, London

Orton writes *Fred and Madge* (play)

Kenneth Halliwell writes *Priapus in the Shrubbery* (novel, now lost)

Orton and Halliwell begin stealing and 'creatively re-arranging' the jackets of books borrowed from the Islington Library

1960 Orton and Halliwell write *The Boy Hairdresser* (novel)

1961 Orton writes *The Vision of Gombold Proval* (novel, published 1971 as *Head to Toe*)

Orton writes *The Visitors* (play)

1962 *April:* Orton and Halliwell arrested for stealing and defacing library books

May–September: Orton gaoled at H.M. Prison Eastchurch, in Kent, and Halliwell gaoled at H.M. Prison Ford, in Sussex, for stealing and defacing library books

1963 Orton writes *The Boy Hairdresser* (play); revised title: *The Ruffian on the Stair*

Orton writes *Entertaining Mr Sloane*

1964 John Kingsley Orton becomes Joe Orton

6 May: Entertaining Mr Sloane produced at Arts Theatre Club, London

June: Orton writes *The Good and Faithful Servant*

29 June: Entertaining Mr Sloane transfers to Wyndham's Theatre

31 August: The Ruffian on the Stair broadcast on the BBC Third Programme

1964-66 Orton writes *Loot*

1965 Orton writes *The Erpingham Camp*

February: first (failed) production of *Loot*

1966   Orton writes *Funeral Games*
September: second (successful) production
of *Loot*
December: Orton begins writing mature
Diaries

1967   *11 January*: Orton wins *Evening Standard*
Award for Best Play of 1966. On the same
day, Orton receives a letter informing him
that he has also won the *Plays and Players*
Award for Best Play of 1966
Orton writes *What the Butler Saw*
Orton writes *Up Against It* (Beatles
screenplay)
June: under the title *Crimes of Passion*,
Orton's one-act plays *The Ruffian on the
Stair* and *The Erpingham Camp* are produced
at the Royal Court Theatre
9 August: Orton murdered by Kenneth
Halliwell, who then commits suicide

F.C.

*Francesca Coppa is Assistant Professor of English at
Muhlenberg College, where she specialises in British
drama and cultural studies. She has published and
lectured widely on Orton both in Britain and the United
States.*

London

Monday

I think I'm going crazy! At the hair-dresser's Miss Fleur gave me the most awful restyle. Just terrible. When I made the appointment I asked for Miss Betty. I shall refuse to go to Miss Fleur again, she's made me look a dreadful sight. And I did so want to look my best for the audition. I could cry.

The Divine Marquisé, the novel I ordered, was in the bookshop waiting for me this afternoon. I was just dying to read it, but mother snatched it off me directly I got in. It all seems so utterly depressing. I have made up my mind that I shall not allow mother to ruin this book for me. I won't listen when she reads the interesting bits. Mother really is sickening. My God! How awful everything is. No romance – no real romance, I mean. I'd give seven years of my life to be swept off my feet by a handsome stranger – like Pompadour in *The Divine Marquisé*.

Well I certainly hope this diary never falls into anyone else's hands – wouldn't it be embarrassing for an unknown person to read a girl's most intimate thoughts?

Thelma came to tea with the *most* gorgeous man. I can't imagine what men see in Thelma. She's quite plain – at least she isn't what one would call beautiful – and yet she can't go into the street without some man making a pass at her. Nobody ever makes a pass at me. Not that I care. I just happen to be the intellectual type. After all Thelma may have a better figure, but when it comes down to brains there just isn't any doubt who wins. I feel sorry for her sometimes. The other day she practically admitted she'd got the worst of the bargain.

'Susan,' she said, 'I wish I could read all these intellectual books.'

'There's nothing to it,' I said.

'I'd be afraid, reading all those brainy books, I might lose my mind.'

I smiled and thought that nobody can lose what they don't own.

Thelma is going to the audition too. Apparently just everyone saw that advertisement. Thelma, Joy, June and Hetty are all going. After Thelma left I went upstairs to mother's room and looked for my book. No use, though. Mother has completely hidden it away. Really, isn't she the limit!

Tuesday

For the audition I wore a 'back interest' dress in Jersey romaine with a soft high neckline in front plunging into a loose cowl at the back. Thelma was quite surprised when she saw me. Vivian Sorsby was there – in fact almost everyone seemed to have turned up. Thelma had the *most* heavenly man with her. As I say, I just don't understand.

Vivian had on a lovely green dress with floating panniers, and the latest scent: Tabu (the forbidden fragrance). She certainly did smell nice. She's just had some thrilling news. Rank want her for a tiny part in a new film, about a young man who for love gives up respectability and takes to a life of crime, gets caught, goes to prison, comes out and becomes a police informer, and through this meets a violent end. Vivian isn't sure yet what her part is to be, but I'm thrilled for her.

We all went to the Blue Raisin afterwards for coffee – just like old times.

Long talk with Vivian who has taken a terribly interesting job in the lamp department at Harrods. She's been simply swamped with offers from television to advertise something or other. And now – well Rank want her. So depressed. Nothing, simply nothing, ever happens to me. Told Thelma how lucky Vivian was and she said: 'If she's so lucky why is she working in Harrods lamp department?'

Arrived home at half past six more dead than alive. Mother has lent *The Divine Marquisé* to Mrs Lee-Baxter.

Wednesday

Met Thelma and Vivian Sorsby again today. Vivian had on that old green dress with the panniers. Simply no news about the audition. Everyone in a perfect frenzy of excitement. I woke up in the night and felt so hungry with worry I just had to go into the kitchen for a cracker biscuit and a glass of milk. The Maharani would be furious if she knew how I neglect my diet. Vivian goes to Norman Savidge, psychologist, hypnotherapist and figure consultant. She says you can command attention and acquire irresistible appeal by improving your figure, and that Mr Savidge just hypnotises her and she loses pounds.

Mother has gone to stay with Mrs Lee-Baxter for the weekend. I invited Monty Woodward, Vivian, Thelma and Joy round for drinks. Told Thelma to bring that absolutely gorgeous man with her. Wrote a few pages of my play before tea and read a little of it to Monty Woodward over the telephone. He said I was developing into the wisest woman of the extra-civilised world. Honestly he is a scream. I simply can't repeat his funniest joke.

Letter from the Rainier Revuebar confirming my request for an audition and fixing one for Thursday. Rang Miss Betty for an appointment.

The gang came round at eight and didn't go away till nearly three. Monty Woodward sang 'Lover' to the man from the basement who came up to complain of the noise. He's a scream. We all played that game where you pretend to be people in history. Monty Woodward borrowed Vivian's dress and my old pink hat and was Lucrezia Borgia offering poison. I just can't understand why anyone as funny as Monty Woodward doesn't get more work.

Thelma called, and we went to the Academy to see *Hunger*. I insisted. After all one can't spend every afternoon doing nothing. It was an interesting film – at least – well, to be quite frank (and who, for Heaven's sake, is there to read this), I had forgotten my glasses and couldn't read the sub-titles. Thelma said she enjoyed it though.

No news yet of the audition. Nearly dead with suspense. Told Thelma about my interview Thursday with the Rainier Revuebar. She was really thrilled for me. So sweet of her. I do so hope I get something soon. Life seems so drab, so squalid. Very depressed.

Mother rang, said she was staying with Mrs Lee-Baxter for another couple of days. I told her to post *The Divine Marquisé* to me if Mrs Lee-Baxter had finished with it.

Arranged to go to the Blue Raisin with Monty Woodward. He's so unexpected. I mean – well, he just sweeps you off your feet. Rings me up and asks can he take me out. I tried to put him off but what can you do? The Blue Raisin is the most elegant eating place I know. So romantic too. There is a glass roof and the moon as big as a hula-hoop floating above.

Monty Woodward just fascinates me. He went to the band and asked if they would play something for him.

'Of course,' they said.

Well then (can you imagine) Monty told them that the mating call of the bull alligator can be imitated by blowing B-flat two octaves below middle G, and would they do it please? It just couldn't happen with anyone but Monty Woodward.

Arrived home to find telegram from mother who has decided to come home to-morrow. I can't think with thinking about the audition. The Maharani told me that she wouldn't take another scrap of interest in me if I didn't stick to my diet. Feel so weary of it all.

Was woken up at four a.m. by a dreadful ringing upon the door. It was mother. She has had the most fearful row with Mrs Lee-Baxter and was practically ordered to leave. I couldn't make head nor tail of the story. Was so tired. Slept till ten-thirty. Mother definitely finished with Mrs Lee-Baxter. I asked if she had remembered to bring *The Divine Marquisé* back with her. No. Mrs Lee-Baxter has lent it to a friend who hasn't returned it. Simply furious! Shall have to order another copy.

A very sad happening is taking place during the middle of next month. They are closing down the Blue Raisin! Vivian Sorsby broke the news to me. She said that the club is being closed for 'several reasons'. Isn't life sad? I mean there we were, Monty Woodward and I, enjoying ourselves and all the time the Blue Raisin was going to be closed down. Honestly I could cry. You sometimes wonder what's the point of it all.

Delicious party at Sheila Gribble's. Everyone was there – Thelma, Joy, June, Vivian Sorsby and of course Monty Woodward. I heard about the party from Vivian – well I simply knew Sheila simply *must* have meant to invite me so I went along with Vivian. Absolutely the most marvellous party. We played that game where everyone has to pretend to be some character in history. Monty Woodward borrowed Sheila's dressing-gown and my ear-rings and was Cleopatra; then he sang 'Lover' to Frank Thompson who hates him (everyone says so). Monty Woodward is going to be discovered some day. I mean – well just everybody admits he's the funniest thing on two legs.

Long talk with Thelma who tells me that Frank Thompson is going to Hollywood end of next month to write the script of a film, about a doctor who thinks she may be accused of murdering the man whose bad character she has accidentally discovered. Lovely things keep happening to all sorts of people, but never to me. I'm fated, I think, always to be left behind.

Sheila Gribble had a record of 'Suddenly it's Moonlight', the hit song from the new musical. Told Sheila it was just the thing I'd been looking for. Intend to sing it at my audition for the Rainier Revuebar.

Sheila said: 'The Rainier Revuebar?'

I said: 'Didn't you know? I had a letter from them the other day. I don't mind telling you I'm thrilled to death about it.'

Sheila said: 'Daaarling. The Rainier Revuebar.'

I said: 'It's a great chance for me if I get a job, only I'm worried about my lack of experience.'

Sheila said: 'Daaarling! Experience? What kind of acting do you think they want on the new mirrored stage? Lady Macbeth?'

Sheila Gribble is just a cat. I certainly shan't let myself be taken to any more of her parties. Quite a few people there I didn't know and I wouldn't want to know. Where Sheila finds them is a mystery to me. Frank Thompson and Thelma left early and I had to take Monty Woodward home – he was feeling ill.

Laddered my stockings, broke two of my nails and had Dubonnet spilled over my Madge Chard hat. Life is simply sickening sometimes.

Thursday

Oh dear I knew this was going to happen. I was talking to Thelma about the audition and she said that they are in rehearsal, have been for days now. So I suppose it must mean that they are not going to get in touch with me at all. I should have expected this, but I did so hope I'd be chosen. I looked at my watch and said: 'I'll have to go now, Thelma.'

Of course she wanted to know why. Isn't it peculiar the way people are so inquisitive. I said: 'I'm going to see Monty Woodward, he was feeling ill and I had to take him home last night.'

Thelma said: 'I've nothing on. I'll come too.'

Thelma is my dearest friend and I would do anything for her, but sometimes – Oh well.

We caught a bus because it was raining. For the first few seconds after entering the room we couldn't speak. We were suffocated by cigarette smoke. Monty was sitting at the table writing a letter to the *Radio Times* suggesting *The Divine Marquisé* as a Sunday-night serial.

It would be quite a good idea really. I hadn't thought of it as a serial but what a good one it would make. Monty was using the only chair. 'Take a seat on the bed,' he said. From where I sat I could see, pasted on the wall, a photograph of Monty cut from a magazine. Underneath it said: 'That fast up and coming young actor Monty Woodward, who has just finished a major role in *Guess What*, has now landed a plum role in a new British film comedy *The Lady Tickle*. Monty is being talked about in certain circles as one of the biggest comedy "finds" for some time.'

I had no idea Monty Woodward was so successful, and I told him so.

He closed those bedroom eyes of his and said: 'You could be a success too, Susan, if you went about it the right way!'

'What *is* the right way?' I said.

'Let me show you.'

He put a little lamp-shade on my head,

lowered my neckline and draped a bed-spread round me. You know, as if he were creating something. 'Beauty, beauty,' he murmured. I can understand why Monty is successful – he's a natural comedian.

We went out for a drink when Monty had finished his letter. On the stairs we passed Bob Kennedy (Monty's flat-mate) with a black eye. He had been present at one of the 'unofficial' entertainments at the Blue Raisin. He looked awful. I was rather afraid he was going to make a pass at me, he was so drunk.

'Where are you three going?' he said.

'For a drink,' I said, 'any objection?' I said this because I was tired of him staring at me as though I were a piece of dead meat.

'Mind if I come along?'

'Why should I mind?' I said.

He should have been in bed, but what can you do? We all got outside somehow. Bob stepped suddenly into a puddle, almost overbalanced, and then looked around to see if anyone had noticed him do so.

'Don't you think you ought to be in bed?' I said.

He leered at me and said: 'Do you?'

We went into a pub and ordered Guinness. Bob Kennedy leant against the counter, drank his Guinness, ordered another, talked to the barmaid, drank his Guinness, and stared at me. I stared back into his little blackcurrant eyes and he said: 'Are you any relation to Peachy Wainwright?'

'I've never heard of him,' I said.

I didn't believe there was such a person. I looked at my watch and said I ought to be going.

'Why where are you going?' he said.

'I don't think it concerns you,' I said.

'How do you know whether it concerns me or not?'

'If you must know,' I said, giving him a sort of cold smile, 'I have an appointment with my hairdresser and I don't want to be late.'

He peeled the cigarette stump he was smoking away from his lip and ground it into an ash-tray. Behind the baby-face, far down, there lay a deep nihilism. I was convinced of that. He was unhappy, you could just tell, but I bet he couldn't remember now why he was unhappy.

'Are you satisfied?' I said, trying not to sound too angry.

He screwed his eyes round to the barmaid and ordered four more Guinnesses. Thelma began to powder her nose. There was a long, uncomfortable silence while the barmaid brought the bottles, unstoppered them, reached for the glasses, filled each one slowly, took the ten shilling note Bob Kennedy gave her and returned the change. I took a tiny sip of my drink and coughed.

Thelma said: 'Monty, would you let me borrow your copy of *The Divine Marquisé*?'

'Do you think your mother will let you read that kind of book?' Monty said.

'It's not too highbrow is it?'

'Wait till you read it.'

'I'm not a highbrow,' Thelma said.

I looked in the mirror and saw that I was getting red in the face, partly with drinking, partly the stuffiness of the atmosphere, and partly annoyance. I had made a mental note to ask Monty for the loan of *The Divine Marquisé* myself. The bookshops all seem to be sold out, not a copy to be had anywhere.

Of course it is the best seller of the decade ...
Suddenly I noticed the time and nearly
screamed.

'My God!' I said, 'It's two o'clock. I must
go.'

Monty Woodward then said the funniest
thing I have ever heard, but I can't repeat it
in case anybody happened to read this.
Thelma and I left Monty Woodward and Bob
and opened the door into the street. It was
raining. We stepped back to let a bus pass.

'My handbag,' I said to Thelma, 'I've left it
behind.'

I went back into the bar, Monty was
talking to a man in a trilby. 'It's a temptation
devoutly to be missed,' he was saying. I
picked up my bag without him having seen
me. Bob Kennedy seemed to have disappeared. The tube station was just around
the corner. Everywhere was bright and
empty, no one about and a train just arriving.
The lights of the approaching train
beat against the walls and I could see
Thelma quite clearly. I still don't understand.
The doors opened, we got in, the doors
closed, the train started.

At the hairdresser's I said goodbye to Thelma and went into a booth with Miss Betty. I had a restyle, shampoo and set. When I glanced into the mirror afterwards I had quite a shock – my face was so red, and what Miss Betty thought she had done to my hair I can't imagine. It looked like an old mop! Even Miss Fleur couldn't have been worse. I felt really angry and didn't bother to tip Miss Betty.

The sun was shining as I arrived at the Rainier Revuebar in Dean Street. It was a small place – from the outside anyway. A big sign said

RAINIER REVUEBAR

in enormous letters. Underneath in smaller letters it said:

Intimate – Sexciting – Non-stop
Fabulous sex-kittens and cats!
Starting soon. Daring new production. New girls.
GUEST STAR
Düsseldorf's own
Countess Sirie von Blumenghast
(Eighteen sensational poses
never displayed before!)

I stepped back to allow an old man pushing a child's pram to pass when suddenly I heard a sound like thunder. I seemed to be spinning in the air, the wall ran to meet me and everything went bang. I felt as if I were going to be sick, then I fainted.

My first thoughts upon opening my eyes were that I must be dead. I was lying on a table, somebody said: 'Here, drink this,' a glass was placed in my hand and guided to my mouth. It was brandy. I felt a burning sensation in my throat, coughed, gave the man the glass back and struggled to sit up.

'Keep calm,' I heard a gentle voice say, 'keep calm. You'll be alright now.'

The man that spoke was nearer fifty than forty, tall, elegant and cool-looking. He had grey hair and a moustache which looked as if it had been chromium-plated. His voice had the faintest trace of an accent, but I couldn't be sure whether it was foreign or provincial. Just above his right eyebrow was a scar, red and shaped like an ace of spades.

'What happened?' I said.

'I'm afraid I knocked you over, you stepped back and – ' I gave a shudder ' –

lucky I wasn't travelling at a greater speed, Miss . . . '

'Hope,' I said, 'Susan Hope.'

The walls around us were painted with heavy, thick-looking cyclamen paint, the doors were silvered and the ceiling was sprinkled with stars. I couldn't imagine where I was. I got up from the table and, in turning, noticed a stage lined with mirrors. Then I realised.

'Is this the Rainier Revuebar?' I said.

'Yes.'

'I have an appointment with Mr Fitz-maurice.'

The man smiled and I could almost see the back of his throat. 'I am Mr Fitzmaurice,' he said.

There didn't seem much to say to this. Mr Fitzmaurice said: 'Are you feeling well enough to take the audition?'

'Oh yes,' I said, 'I feel fine.'

He patted my arm. 'Very well, Miss Hope, if you go through the little door you see over there and ask Chris for some lights we'll begin. Have you brought your music?'

I said I had and he smiled again and held

my hand. 'You have beautiful hands,' he said.

I said: 'Glad you think so,' very softly because I didn't want him to think I was being sarcastic.

'Yes, very beautiful,' then, as if recollecting himself, he spoke to the woman seated at the piano in a corner of the room. 'Here, Lottie, can you play this?'

She caught my roll of music which Mr Fitzmaurice had thrown over to her, looked at it and said: 'I could play this under the influence.'

I thought that that was probably how she usually played, but I merely asked her not to play too fast and left the room. At the top of the stairs I found a man reading the *Daily Mirror*.

'Are you Chris?' I said.

He looked me up and down, folded up the *Mirror*, carefully put it away and lit a cigarette before he spoke. 'Yes,' he said.

'Mr Fitzmaurice wants some light. I'm going to have an audition.'

He said: 'Are you going to strip?' When I told him I wasn't he looked disappointed.

'Go on,' he said, 'Fitzmaurice likes them that show willing.'

'I'm not that willing,' I said, feeling annoyed at having to make such a cheap remark.

He ignored this and began to climb up an iron ladder fixed to the wall. 'Through there,' he muttered out of the corner of his mouth.

'What?'

'Go through there,' he said, disappearing into the electrician's loft.

People are so inconsiderate. I mean – well, he just vanished leaving me staring at a blank wall.

I began to wish I hadn't either heard of or seen the Rainier Revuebar. It took me another two minutes to find the door tucked away behind a corner. I thought the whole thing absolutely death-like – and my hip was beginning to throb where Mr Fitzmaurice's car had bumped me. I pushed at the door, but it wouldn't open, so I pulled and it still refused to move. It was locked. Really, I thought, this is like a mad-house. Going to the bottom of the iron ladder

I called loudly, demanding to know why the door wasn't open. Silence. No reply at all. So I went back to the door and literally screamed through it. After a couple of seconds it opened and Lottie appeared.

She said: 'What are you making such a bloody racket about?'

'I couldn't get in.'

'Why didn't you ask Chris?'

'I couldn't make him hear.'

She gave a snort like a horse diving into a bag of oats and marched across the stage back to her piano.

'Do I begin now?' I said.

There was no reply.

'Do I begin now?' I shouted.

Lottie played a deafening chord and said: 'Let's get this straight, Hope, I couldn't care less what you do – Bunny's gone for a wet, so you'd better keep quiet till he gets back.'

I sat upon a chair and waited. Chris was amusing himself by flooding the stage alternately with pink and green light. After what seemed like three hours Mr Fitzmaurice returned, clapped his hands, yelled to Chris – who promptly swilled the stage with regulation pink – and told me to begin.

Lottie was good. It surprised me to find she even knew bass from treble, which she did and a lot more besides. I began to sing, feeling miserable and nervous:

> *Suddenly it's Moonlight,*
> *Suddenly it's Night-time,*
> *Suddenly your cheeks glow,*
> *And your eyes meet mine . . .*

Oh what's the use, I thought, all this just to hear him say: 'Thank you, Miss Hope, I'll get in touch with you.' My hip was giving me hell, I was dazzled by the light, I blinked, my voice slipped off key, I paused as indicated in the music, Lottie played on.

'Can you take it a shade faster, Miss Hope?' Mr Fitzmaurice's voice sepulchrally enquired. I nodded.

> *. . . you take my hand,*
> *I understand.*
> *Suddenly it's Moonlight,*
> *And I'm in love.*

The music came to an abrupt end. I waited for the old familiar sentence. It didn't come. Instead Mr Fitzmaurice advanced towards me, threading his way among the tables.

What kind of a figure have you got?' he said. I stared at him. 'Is it all your own?'

'Every bit,' I said.

'No foam rubber?' I shook my head. 'Alright. Now I'm prepared to give you a job – we're in the middle of rehearsal at the moment so I shall expect to see you at ten-thirty sharp tomorrow. And I mean sharp, not ten-forty or eleven. Understand?' I couldn't say a word so I just sort of looked reliable. He turned to Lottie. 'Take her to the office, sweetie, give her the usual contract will you?'

I was just too utterly amazed. Like that. A job. Honestly you don't know when your luck is turning. I almost danced after Lottie to the office. And what an office it was. Mr Fitzmaurice used it more as a general living-room, he even slept there sometimes. In one corner was a screen decorated with photographs cut from Nature magazines, behind this was a tap and washbasin. In the sink was a cup that had been employed as a shaving mug and was smeared with hair and Gibbs easy-shaving stick. Lottie rummaged about in a drawer producing pencils, pens, sheaves of papers and even a brassiere edged with pink lace before she found what she wanted. I sat opposite her while she explained about salary, conditions of employment and – oh, hundreds of things. She pushed a fountain pen towards me and I signed a six-months contract terminable on either side by a fortnight's notice.

'Can I ask you something,' I said.

'Go ahead.'

I said: 'Do I – I mean – well, what do I *wear*? It isn't nude, is it?'

Her nostrils flared and did a crazy kind of jig, she dilated the pupils of her eyes and began to suck in air as though she had just escaped strangulation.

'Get this straight, Hope,' she said, 'there is only one person here who is allowed to show what the Lord gave her, and that is Sirie von Blumenghast. If she catches you exposing so much as a toe nail that isn't in the script you're out.'

'That's alright,' I said, 'I don't want to take anything off, I – '

She cut me short with a wave of her hand. 'Something else I've got to tell you, Hope.' Pausing for a moment she gathered up her copy of the contract and stuffed it into a top drawer. I folded my own copy and put it into my handbag. 'For God's sake have something done to your hair. There's a pretty decent place round the corner, ask for Miss Fleur, she'll put you right.'

I said I'd have a restyle before the show opened. Lottie yawned and said: 'I've had enough of this for a bit, like to come and have a Turkish? It'll while away a couple of hours, then you could see the show – see what kind of thing we do.'

'I've a date,' I said.

'Some other time then?'

I went out into Dean Street in a perfect frenzy of emotion. Rang Thelma and Vivian Sorsby, who just yelled with delight for me. Long talk with Vivian, who invited me over to her place for a long talk. I keep bubbling all the time. My heart feels like a glass of liver salts.

Arrived home to find my copy of *The Divine Marquisé* had been sent through the post by Mrs Lee-Baxter. I'm really not interested in reading now, though.

Wednesday

What a week! Too deliriously happy. Met Thelma once, and Monty Woodward a couple of times. I'm worried about Monty – so afraid he may be getting serious about me. Saw Bob Kennedy last night. He looked awful, and his lip was cut. How a nice person like Monty Woodward can go around with someone of Bob Kennedy's calibre is beyond me.

Quite unexpected letter from dear Sheldon Hunt. It was a surprise. I haven't heard from him since mother and I were on the continent over a year ago. He said:

Dear Susan,
By this time you've probably forgotten me and used up all the little pills I gave you to take away the blues. It was that time when you were at the Von Steuben in Wiesbaden, remember now, Sheldon Hunt?
My thoughts have wandered to you, and the

few short hours we knew each other, many times since I've been back in America. Have you thought about coming here to work at all? I'm going to see an agent tomorrow about other English friends of mine that want to work here, and I will mention you. Let me know if you are interested.

No doubt about it, I really miss Europe. If possible I shall get a job at a French or Italian studio. It's amazing how a place can get under your skin and cause you to have longings for it.

Drop me a line. Let me know how you are.

Fondly, Sheldon

Imagine Sheldon Hunt remembering me. I must write to him, if I ever find the time. Rehearsals are nearly over for the revue, called *Little by Little*. Simply everyone is coming on the first night; Thelma, Vivian Sorsby, Monty Woodward, June and Joy have all promised to come and give me a big cheer. How sweet. I talk sometimes at gang parties until my throat is dry – telling people who just *must* know exactly what the scenes are like. My favourite (it's sensational) is the one where the curtains open and we girls are discovered sitting on top of enormous red pillar boxes singing like mad. The high spot, of course, is the item called 'Tearing off a Strip'. The Countess Sirie von Blumenghast is superb – she's a really great artist, and so intelligent.

I'm really beginning to like Lottie, too. She has a genuine 24-carat gold heart, though she doesn't often show it. I said to her, after rehearsal one day: 'Have you been here long?'

She locked the piano lid. 'Long enough,' she said.

'I just adore it.'

She favoured me with a long, withering stare and gave a sort of half-snarl, like a crocodile about to attack. 'You would,' she said.

'If you don't like it, why don't you leave?'

'How do you know I'm not going to?'

'I don't.'

'As a matter of fact I've told Bunny to find himself a new pianist.'

'You're leaving?'

'End of the week.'

I was really stunned. 'But – Lottie, who will play for us?' I said.

'It's quite amazing to me, Hope, how you can look so stupid and be so stupid,' she said, with a loud, braying intonation. 'Girls who look as stupid as you do are often exceptionally intelligent.'

I sighed. 'I'm sorry,' I said, 'it does seem funny, though, you rehearsing us – and now, just when we're almost ready to open – you disappear.'

'Anyone could play a few chords while Sirie Blumenghast takes off her clothes,' she said. 'You know that as well as I do.'

'I suppose it isn't very difficult.' I followed her along to the office where she began to make a cup of tea. 'What are you going to do?' I said.

'I'm taking charge of a few girls for the Monteith woman.'

'Who?'

'Liz Monteith.'

'Who's she?'

For a moment she watched a pigeon fluttering down the street between the lamp-posts. 'She owns one or two clubs in America. Very well off. Bloated plutocrats and all that,' she said.

'How does she make her money, from these clubs?'

'God, no. She's the daughter of Sir somebody or other, I dunno. Sugar?'

I nodded. 'What's this job you're doing for her?'

She didn't speak while she tipped water into the pot, then she gave a high, rasping noise, which passed with her for a laugh. 'She's opening a new place in Mareposa, in Mexico, near the U.S. border. I'm an escort. I just take the little angels across, see there's no trouble (you know what some people are) then back here again. Sea, fresh air, sunshine. Who could ask for anything more. *And* I get paid for it. My idea of bliss.'

I watched her burrow among a pile of papers and emerge holding a plate with two jam tarts on it.

'I do envy you,' I said.

'You'd like to come along?'

'Like to? Oh, Lottie, darling you've no idea.'

'I might be able to manage it,' she said, burying her long nose into a tart. I remembered something, my face must have showed it for she said: 'What's the matter now?'

I said: 'I've just had the most ghastly thought – my contract, I have to give a fortnight's notice and you're leaving at the end of the week.'

For maybe a minute we sat drinking tea in complete silence. 'We'll soon fix that,' Lottie said at last, rising and stepping across to a battered looking filing cabinet. She licked her thumb and ruffled through a line of contracts, wrinkling her forehead until she had found what she was looking for. 'Here it is,' she said, sliding a contract across the table.

'What am I supposed to do with it?'

'I dunno. Burn it. Here give it to me.'

She opened the window and leaned out to see if anyone were in the yard. After finding the place deserted she took a cigarette lighter from her pocket, put the contract on the window-sill, held it down with a steel ruler, and carefully set fire to each corner. The flames rose higher, crawled up the ruler and died away until only a pile of charred, blackened paper remained. Lottie scattered the ashes and closed the window.

'There we are. Bunny'll never know,' she said.

'What about –' I looked around me in case Mr Fitzmaurice were listening ' – Mareposa?'

'Don't you worry about that, I'll have a talk with Liz about you. She'll want to see what kind of a girl you are, give you the once over, of course. But everything'll be OK.' She dropped into the chair beside me. 'Now, feel like a Turkish?'

I felt terrible having to turn her down a second time, but I'd promised to meet mother. I said: 'I can't, Lottie, I'm sorry.'

Her eyebrows rose sharply. 'I must say, Hope, you're pretty bloody standoffish. I *have* practically got you the job of a lifetime.'

This made me feel angry, with myself for being ungrateful, and with Lottie for making me feel so. I said impatiently: 'Look I can't – not now. When we get to Mareposa I'll spend a week in a Turkish Bath with you, if you like.'

Her eyebrows did a shimmy, rose another inch and nearly disappeared into her hairline, she showed the whites of her eyes and gave a faint, asthmatic cough. I finished my tea, thanked her for everything and left. Before I did so I opened the window to see what remained of my contract. It had been blown away. I still had my own copy of it, though – if the worst came to the worst.

Monday

I haven't put anything in my diary for absolute ages. Now I shall have to write practically all day if I want to catch up.

Three days after Lottie burned my contract in the office of the Rainier Revuebar she drove me down to Kingsleigh, the village in Surrey where Miss Monteith and her sister lived. It was a perfect day, the sky a deep blue faintly haired over with cloud, nothing spectacular just ordinary, but it seemed wonderful. Here I was, going to meet the woman who would give me a fabulous job. And it was happening to me. Honestly I had to pinch myself to believe it. I couldn't have been happier. The living seemed to be easy and the landscaping all that I could wish. We had chosen Saturday to call on Miss Monteith because I had no rehearsal to attend and, as the current show didn't begin until five-thirty, Lottie was free for the day.

At the end of half an hour we approached Kingsleigh and drew up beside a driveway. I got out to open the white-painted gate, on it in black lettering was written, JESMOND, on the gatepost a brass plate announced that Miss Elizabeth and Miss Sylvia Monteith lived there. Lottie opened the car door, I got in, she drove through the gates, got out, closed the gates, opened the car door, got in and we drove up to the house.

At the age of five, when my mother asked me what I wanted to be when I grew up, I'm supposed to have replied that I wanted to be a lady with a house and a fountain. I remembered this because Miss Monteith's house had a fountain, not a very good one – just a fish dribbling water from its mouth as though it were being sick, but I suppose it was the kind of thing I meant. The house had a glass front door, the kind of glass which can be seen out of but not into. We rang the bell. After we had done this a great deal of noise commenced, a dog started to bark, a woman's voice yelled for it to be quiet. It was quiet. Then another sound began, the noise made by high heels on bare wood. Whoever it was clack-clacked the length of the hall shutting doors until she opened the one behind which we were standing.

'Lottie!' she squealed, showing a fine view of all thirty-two teeth, which she snapped shut upon seeing me. 'This is the girl, is it?' she said, in a voice scraped thin and clean. 'Come on in, you must be tired.'

Why she imagined we must be tired at eleven o'clock in the morning, and why she pretended to be so overjoyed upon seeing Lottie when she must have known we were coming is a complete mystery. People are like that. Nerves, I think.

The hall Miss Monteith led us into was quite bare like her voice, polished, anaemic, scraped and clean. The walls were white, the ceilings were white, the woodwork a dull steely blue. We were shown into a cloaks cupboard a little bigger than the Albert Hall where Miss Monteith snatched my hat and coat, hung them on a peg, and quick-marched me into a sitting-room. Before I could even speak a larger than life-sized replica of the Hound of the Baskervilles sprang at my throat. I screamed. Miss Monteith rushed forward and chased it out of the room. I could hear her voice calling 'Sylvie, look after Macmillan' down the hall and, faintly, another voice, then some kind of argument.

'He doesn't belong to me.'

'Mumble mumble mumble lock him up somewhere, Sylvie mumble mumble.'

A thud, a tinkle of glass, the dog barking loud enough to shatter all the windows in the house, and then: 'Sylvie, do something can't you. Mumble mumble mumble mumble mumble mumble mumble. Really!! Mumble mumble mumble sick and tired of mumble mumble. It's absolutely unforgivable – '

Lottie got up and closed the door. It was closed for a second and then opened again. Miss Monteith had re-entered.

She was about as tall as a woman can be without having beans grow up her. She had hair which, though straight once, now curled out of sheer desperation after having been permanently waved each month since nineteen twenty. A rosebud mouth and heavy eyebrows jutting out like balconies over a pair of grape-black eyes completed the picture.

She gave a clever imitation of a smile and said: 'Wonderful weather you've brought with you.'

Lottie looked at her and then at the room, momentarily raped of speech. It would have been a nice room once. Long and elegant, it yearned towards the French windows and garden as if trying to escape from the rest of the house. My first guess upon seeing it was that the Misses Monteith were about to leave Jesmond, all their furniture having been already sent ahead. I was wrong. A weary green carpet stretched, flat and unending as the pampas, from window to door, from fireplace to wall, without hardly ever encountering any other object. A few hard-looking chairs and a settle were about all there was in the room.

'I'll have a talk with you later, Susan,' Miss Monteith said, her face showing the strain of friendship attempted. 'I don't want to frighten you the moment you arrive.'

I smiled, incoherently expressing my thanks.

The next thing she did was unexpected. 'Cigarette?' she said, and pulled a box from under the single cushion placed on the settle. I sympathised with her, though. Where else *could* you keep anything in a room with no furniture? I looked at her again, hoping she might produce a three-course meal from beneath her skirt. She wore a tunic in cigar-brown blanket-weave wool with a wide, square neckline introducing a low décolletage to daylight. What she wore underneath was her secret.

Lottie spoke now for the first time since the squeals at the door. 'God!' she said, 'whatever have you done to this room? It looks like a ladies' lavatory.'

Miss Monteith passed a sneer-smile round her face. She said: 'It's Sylvie, I can't do anything with her. She read a perfectly bloody article in the Sunday Times by some clod who said it was *the* latest thing to have your rooms bare, just a few things pinched from monasteries.'

She began to kneel upon the carpet. I thought the mention of monasteries had reminded her to pray until she wrenched open the drawers between seat and floor on the settle and produced an ash-tray.

'It was all I could do to stop her taking down the curtains,' she said.

Lottie said: 'I'll have a talk with her if you like.'

'Oh don't, I'm terrified she might start on the bedrooms. I have to go to bed now if I want to be comfy.'

'Is every room like this?' I said.

She edged the ash-tray towards me. 'Except the bedrooms.'

Out of the corner of my eye, I saw that Lottie was examining a scratched old cupboard.

'Forty quid that cost me,' said Miss Monteith, as if she foresaw the ruin of civilisation. 'I don't know what I'm going to do with Sylvie.'

Lottie said: 'Where's the Victoriana?'

'Upstairs. The attics are full of stuffed birds, wax fruit, and those nasty china figurines. I'm seriously thinking, Lottie, of dividing the house into two flats, then she can decorate and re-decorate in whatever fashion she chooses.'

She puffed angrily at her cigarette for a minute or two. I hoped she had finished. She hadn't.

'Look at that Louis Quatorze or Quinze stuff – all horrid buhl and gilding – we didn't get a half of what we paid for it when she sold it to make room for the wax fruits.'

Lottie said: 'I noticed the door was new.'

Miss Monteith gave a despairing wail. 'Horrid, simply foul, isn't it? Why we can't have a sensible door made of wood, I don't know. And you should see the dining-room! To be quite frank, Lottie, I wouldn't have been surprised if she'd wanted nothing but mats and screens.'

Lottie rumbled with laughter. 'I'm not eating anything out of a bowl with chopsticks,' she said.

We sat in silence watching cigarette smoke drift towards the open window and out into the garden. Miss Monteith was getting ready for another philippic when the door opened.

I thought at first Bela Lugosi had claimed another victim, then a smiling vision skimmed over the carpet, like a tea-cosy on casters, as it called: 'Lottie, darling!' The voice, which I suspected at certain times and in some registers was beyond the range of human hearing, belonged to a creature with beige-coloured skin who, after being introduced, stared at me out of eyes which crawled from beneath wrinkled lids like uneasy snails. She wore her dull black hair very thin and, it occurred to me, she was trying to keep up with the room. We had hardly begun to be polite to each other when she rose and ran from the room, returning breathless to explain that she 'had left Macmillan in the garden unleashed.' Something told me that Miss Monteith could get her sister certified if she played her cards right.

'Do you like my room?' Sylvie asked, casting prudish glances at the ash-tray and cigarettes upon the settle.

'No,' Lottie said.

Sylvie said: 'Cecil Beaton recommended it', as if she had dozens of famous friends who periodically told her to empty and fill her house with furniture.

'Poor old Liz has just been telling us about all this,' Lottie said, indicating 'all this' with a wave. 'I think it's a rotten idea, Sylvie, even worse than all that buhl muck – which is saying something.'

Sylvie pouted like a little girl. 'Jean likes it,' she said.

'Oh, Jean!' This was from Miss Monteith who had just begun to light another cigarette.

'She doesn't often like things.'

Miss Monteith said, 'I'm not going to argue,' opened the French window wider and emptied the ashtray outside. She brought it back, placed it carefully between us on the settle and lapsed into silence. Morosely, for the next fifteen minutes, she stared into the distance at the bare walls. Sylvie told us about a luxurious new infra-red cooker she'd bought, and when this failed to interest anyone, left the room.

Lottie said: 'Who's this Jean?'

'Vicar's sister-in-law,' said Miss Monteith.

A silence, lasting so long that I began to feel worried, descended upon us. I was bored. I had nothing to do, there was nothing to look at in the room, the sky had clouded over and a cold wind started to blow through the room.

Miss Monteith got up and closed the window. 'Can you amuse yourself, Lottie, while I have a chat to Susan?' she said.

'Not in this room,' Lottie said.

Miss Monteith made a face. 'You're free to go anywhere you like. Tell me if you find a comfortable chair.'

She led the way across the hall. I could hear Macmillan barking somewhere near and glanced nervously behind me. I hoped he was on a lead. We tramped up the stairs, which rang hollowly when they didn't creak. A window on the first landing was open. I caught a glimpse of the fish-fountain before Miss Monteith hurried past. In front of a clean door, stripped of paint and un-polished, we paused for Miss Monteith to get her breath back and entered. There was a big desk with nothing on it in the centre of the room, two windows gave onto a view which must have looked nice under snow, a lot of bookcases, which ought to have concealed secret passages, lined the walls. I found myself treading carefully: my heels still made a racket on the wooden floor. I had time to wonder in what way Miss Monteith had prevented her sister from tearing up the carpet in the sitting-room before the questioning began.

She said: 'How old are you, Susan?'

'Twenty-two,' I said.

Miss Monteith produced a notebook and pencil out of thin air and began to scribble, then she looked at me and said: 'Has Lottie told you the kind of girl I want?'

'No,' I said.

'Well I'm opening a new place in Mareposa – a couple of hundred miles from the U.S. border. I'm telling you this because you're sure to find it out sooner or later. If I decide to employ you I shall want a two-year contract signed. Is that quite clear?'

'Yes.'

'I don't want to ship a dozen girls out there and have them sneaking off to seek their fortunes in Hollywood, or some such nonsense.'

'I won't,' I said, though the idea had occurred to me.

'Alright. I'm taking Lottie's word for your talent, I think I can trust her. She says you've a nice voice.'

I gave a smile which I hope conveyed an impression of great talent, but modestly concealed.

'It's pretty simple work really,' Miss Monteith said, 'get Lottie to explain all that side of it to you.'

'It's . . . just singing and dancing?'

'Yes. No nude stuff – the authorities are firm about it.' She made a few more notes and then said: 'Have you a passport?'

'Yes,' I said.

'If you let Lottie have it she'll fix you up with visas and anything else you need.'

'You're giving me the job?' I said.

'Yes – now about salary. I can't pay more than thirty a week.'

I tried to look as if thirty pounds a week were just a little more than I was usually offered. I didn't succeed.

Miss Monteith peered anxiously out of the window. 'Of course you'll live with the other girls in the hostel provided. This isn't compulsory but – ' She stared into my eyes. 'I do most strongly advise it. These places abroad are not like English towns.'

'I'll take your word for that,' I said.

'Good. It's a nice place in a respectable district. I'm sure you'll like it.' After a few more scribbles in her book, she said: 'How about your parents?'

'What about them?'

'I know you're over twenty-one, Susan, but I would prefer you to obtain your father's consent.'

'That's going to be difficult,' I said. 'He was blown to pieces over Farringdon Street in 1940.'

She looked suitably impressed, registered sorrow and gave me a they-will-not-grow-old-etc look, then said: 'How about your mother, is she still living?'

'Unless she's been strangled by the milk-boy,' I said.

'Will she object – you'll be away for two years.'

I said: 'Mother and I agreed to call it a day years ago.'

Miss Monteith pressed both of her lips together so tightly that the red part disappeared. I looked out of the window and imagined Mareposa. 'Has it got a beach?' I said, startling Miss Monteith into life again.

'What? Oh – no I'm afraid it hasn't.'

'It doesn't matter.'

Life flowed away from her again, reminding me of a film I'd seen with Thelma in which the vital forces of beautiful girls were drained from them by a devilish machine. Only Miss Monteith wasn't a beautiful girl. Rain hissed against the window panes. I hadn't brought a mack with me and it was my best hat that was locked away in the cloaks cupboard. At least the weather must be better in Mareposa. Unless the rainy season had set in before we arrived. Which reminded me.

'When are we leaving?' I said.

'Early next month. The sixth or seventh, I'll check for you if you like.'

'No. Lottie can tell me.'

Lottie could explain a good deal: why she had already left the Rainier Revue-bar if we weren't due to leave for three weeks, why she'd taken the trouble to burn my contract when I could perfectly easily give Mr Fitzmaurice a fortnight's notice, and quite a few other puzzlements I'd collected.

'I want you to take this card to my agent in London,' Miss Monteith said.

She handed over a card with her name and address on one side and on the other a pencilled note: 'To introduce Miss Hope. Standard contract minus board and lodging. Liz.' How much will she be stinging me for B & L, I thought.

Miss Monteith consulted her notes and flung herself into a curtain speech. 'Your passage is provided for, Susan, and if you stay the whole two years we pay your return fare. If through no fault of your own you have to leave us, or if you prove unsuitable, we furnish a passage to England. We expect a certain amount of goodwill and co-operation. I'm quite sure we shall get on very well – anything you want to know don't hesitate to ask Lottie, or even ring me. Now, shall we go down to luncheon.'

She gave a grade 3b English gentry smile and led the way down the cold, draughty, bare, scrubbed stairs along the white and blue hall into a dining-room that had to be seen to be believed.

A worm-eaten table stood, forlornly, lost

among a waste of whitewash. The windows had no curtains, just Venetian blinds which rattled like crickets in the draught. I sat myself upon a stool in silence and waited for the black bread and water.

Lottie came slowly into the room. 'Where's Sylvie?' she whispered, as though she were in church.

'I don't know,' said Miss Monteith as Sylvie entered, smiling brightly about her.

Surprisingly enough the meal was good: soup, cold roast beef and salad, and apple-pie. Sylvie had no imagination where food was concerned, or else Miss Monteith kept the cooking firmly in her own hands. After luncheon the mysterious Jean arrived, unexpectedly. She was announced by a frenzied barking from Macmillan and an X-film shriek from Sylvie.

I exchanged damp fingers with Jean, we all laughed with her about the merry things the villagers did, prevented Macmillan from massacring Jean's cocker spaniel and then, too exhausted with barks and screams to even say goodbye properly, we tottered to the front door.

'I must say, Liz,' Lottie remarked, leaning against the porch, 'I do see your point about separate flats.'

'I'd have to insist upon the top one,' she said.

'Worth it, though, wouldn't it?'

Miss Monteith did a calculation. 'If this new place pays I'll see.'

'Shouldn't be any "if" about it.'

'New places often take a while to catch on, the local populations are conservative.'

Miss Monteith swung her body inside the door and prepared to say goodbye. 'I'll have to go, Lottie, ring me on Monday, will you?' Lottie nodded. 'Miss Hope has to pay a visit to Lehmann, go with her if you can.' Lottie nodded again. 'I'd come with you to the car but it's drizzling and I'm not as young as I was. 'Bye, Miss Hope.'

Lottie nuzzled her cheek and the door was slammed.

The drive was veiled in rain, rain glistened on the roads, London loomed up to meet us out of a bank of rain. I left Lottie outside the Rainier Revuebar – she was playing there for the last time – and caught the tube home. No one was in when I arrived. I fixed a drink and rang Thelma. She was out. I rang Vivian Sorsby.

I paid a visit to Lehmann, the agent, a few days later. Lottie chaperoned me as far as Lehmann's private office. It had an oval panel of frosted glass with 'Lehmann' in black capitals across it. Lehmann wasn't in when we arrived, his confidential secretary – a girl whose whole outlook on life seemed to have been warped by the strain of working for Lehmann – said: 'He isn't in.'

I said: 'I've an appointment.'

'What name is it, please?' she said, getting ready to jab me with her nail-file.

'Hope.'

'Bob Hope?'

'Yes,' I said.

She presented me with a thin smirk. 'I'm expecting him in at any minute.'

From the look of her pinny that wasn't the only thing she was expecting. I joined Lottie in the corner and said: 'He's out.'

'He's in,' she said.

'But she told me – '

'I've known Lehmann longer than she has, though not on the same terms. He's in.'

Miss Cleverpants pounded her typewriter for maybe a minute, then she rose, ambled for no particular reason into the office, closed the door, opened the door and came out. The intercom buzzed.

'Mr Lehmann will see you now,' she said.

'Where did he come from,' I said, 'out of the inkwell?'

Her lip curled evilly as she put a sheet of paper into the typewriter. I went into Lehmann's office. He was sitting half turned from the window watching the door open. Behind him a cheese sandwich stood on a pile of papers and a cigar smoked gently to itself. Lehmann stood a knife's edge under five foot eight, his skull had been almost laid bare by time and worry. He had everything ready for signing and pushed pen and blotter towards me.

'Miss Hope?' he said, in a whining voice which ought to have been asking for alms.

'Yes,' I said.

The shelf over the fireplace was littered with photographs, cards, bills and circulars. I couldn't recognise anyone in the photographs, although I thought a couple of them might have been Lottie at school. I examined them for a minute or two and then found one accidentally pushed to the back. It showed the Countess Sirie von Blumenghast in a typical pose, underneath was written: 'To darling Lottie, the best pianist ever, in memory of – ' And then a word I couldn't decipher.

'This place is like a bloody pig-sty,' Lottie said, coming into the room with two cups of coffee on a tray.

As I'd been thinking this for some time I said, guiltily: 'Oh, it's not too bad.'

'Good God, Hope, you don't need to be polite with me.'

'I'm not being polite,' I said feebly.

We sipped coffee, it was sweet and had been made with milk. I could hear the cooing of pigeons somewhere. It was so near that I wondered if Lottie kept them in her kitchen. A tousled ginger cat slipped into the room. Then I knew she couldn't keep pigeons. Lottie poured some coffee into her saucer and coaxed the cat to drink it.

'I had no idea you knew the Countess Sirie personally,' I said at last.

Lottie shrugged. 'She's a good scout – over-emotional, like all the Huns, but a real pal after a glass of Pims.'

She picked up a watch with no hands, tried to tell the time from it and put it down again in disgust.

'I shall have to clear out of here when I get back from Mareposa. It sickens me,' she said. 'I've let the place go to pot lately.'

I wasn't in any mood for deprecatory speeches from Lottie. I pretended I wanted to go to the lavatory and slipped out. A man with horn-rimmed glasses leaned against the banisters smoking a Woodbine. Somewhere above an accordion was playing. The man with glasses was still there when I came out of the lavatory.

He said: 'Can you let me have tuppence? I want to make a telephone call, you see, and I only have a fiver on me.'

'I haven't got my bag with me,' I said.

'You could get it, couldn't you?'

'Alright,' I said, thinking that tuppence wouldn't break me and might help him.

Back in the flat Lottie was washing-up and singing in a loud voice. I opened my purse, found I only had sixpence, no coppers at all. I went into the kitchen to ask Lottie.

'Can you change sixpence?' I said.

Her eyebrows did a dance. 'What for?'

'There's a chap outside wants tuppence for the telephone – I've half-promised I'll give it to him.'

Lottie closed her eyes and seemed to be repeating the Paternoster. Quite suddenly she dried her hands upon the glass-cloth, rolled down her sleeves, straightened her hair, went to the door and spat out a volley of the foulest abuse I have ever heard at the waiting man. She came back and closed the door.

'You're too soft-hearted, Hope, that's your trouble,' she said, resuming the washing-up.

'It was only tuppence,' I said.

Lottie's upper lip wriggled like a viper. 'He gets money from everyone. You aren't the first. He makes a living out of it.'

'I'm sorry.'

'How anyone as innocent as you are can

survive in this day and age . . . '

After finishing the washing-up we went to do some of Lottie's shopping and then I had to go home. I called in at the Rainier Revue-bar on my way, to pick up a coat I'd left at rehearsal the previous day. I passed the Countess Sirie in the foyer in a dress which revealed her figure with almost X-ray accuracy. She looked divine, though. I went to the dressing-room, collected my coat and was on my way downstairs when I bumped into Mr Fitzmaurice.

'Miss Hope!' he said, 'there is no rehearsal today.'

'I know,' I said. 'I'm collecting a coat I left here yesterday.'

'Never leave anything about in the dressing-rooms, Miss Hope, the manage-ment cannot be held responsible for articles lost or stolen.'

'I understand that – it's an old coat anyway.'

'Unfortunately the class of girl we some-times have to employ would steal the hat from a scarecrow.'

He guided me towards the entrance as

though I were ninety. He bit his lip, considered, chose his words carefully, and then said: 'Miss Hope, would you like to have dinner with me?'

'Not tonight.'

'I don't mean necessarily tonight – any night. How about Friday?'

'Not Friday. I could manage Thursday.'

'Thursday, then?'

'Yes,' I said, as he pushed me through the door into the street.

He gave my arm a squeeze. 'We could have something to eat, and then do a show.'

'Oh no!' I said, 'Not a show. I'm just too tied up with the one I'm going to be in.'

I hadn't the heart to tell him that I wouldn't be in it for long.

'Well, we'll think of something on Thursday.'

With this promise he left me. I watched him slip away among the crowd and thought what a wonderful man he was. I was still grateful to him for giving me a job, but apart from that I really admired him. After looking in a few shop windows I felt ravenous and went home.

Thelma invited me to a marvellous party. All the gang were there. Just everyone wanted to offer congratulations on my Mareposa job. I had the most frightful scene with Monty Woodward. He wanted to borrow my favourite Madge Chard hat to play some stupid game with. Really, I don't think Monty Woodward nearly as funny as certain people try to make him seem.

Long talk with Bob Kennedy who was looking simply terribly handsome and attractive in a blue-striped denim jacket. He has had his hair, which is the most heavenly blond, cut short. It sticks up from his head like gold wire. Bob told me that he was utterly disillusioned with the theatre and show-business in general. He has taken a job as steward on an ocean-going liner. Sounds exciting.

Vivian Sorsby came to Thelma's party later on. She seemed depressed. I tried to cheer her up, but I felt so happy that I wasn't much use. Vivian was wearing a black and white fine checked worsted jacket and matching skirt. She looked too depressed for words, though.

The gang were wonderful. They sang 'For She's a Jolly Good Fellow' before I left. People are so nice sometimes.

Heard from Vivian Sorsby that *The Divine Marquisé* has been banned in Ireland, also that Hollywood are making a film of it. Talent-scouts are combing the world for a girl who could possibly play Madame de Pompadour. Who could? I thought of all the girls I know but I had to admit that they wouldn't really 'get' Pompadour. Film isn't going to be made for years. Just must see it when it comes out. I simply haven't had time to read the book yet. Everyone says it's superb. So accurate in detail. The authoress is supposed to have spent a night wandering around the Palace of Versailles – just to get the right atmosphere. I'd be afraid of catching cold myself, but it truly is wonderful what people will do for art.

Bob Kennedy saw me home from the party. It was nearly midnight, the streets were deserted. The moon beat down on the pavement and a drunk, lying in a patch of shadow, raised his head, saw we weren't the police and closed his eyes again. The moon was bone-white, picked clean and surgical-looking. The sky over London was titillated yellow by a million street lamps, and the lamp-light and the moon-light mingled into a tide of brightness which engulfed people and buildings, which turned every stone and every piece of flesh into a strange new creation.

'When does your ship sail?' I said to Bob.

'In about a fortnight.'

'What is it called?'

'The Corona del Mar.'

'What does it mean?'

'The Crown of the Sea, I think.'

We crossed the road not even bothering to look left and right. A bus rumbled past the end of the road making a sudden thunder of sound. I shivered.

'Are you cold?' Bob said.

I said: 'A little.'

I thought he was going to take off his jacket and offer it to me. He didn't. We stopped in the shadow of a wall. Bob took out a cigarette, struck a match and held his hands cupped about it to shield it from the wind. He threw the match away. We walked on.

'How did you come to get mixed up with this Mareposa gang?' he said.

'A woman I know – she got me an introduction to Miss Monteith.'

A grin skidded about his face, he peeled the cigarette from his mouth and laughed. 'That's why I'm giving it up,' he said.

'What?'

'Why don't you do something with your head before it turns to powder and blows away?'

'I don't know what you mean.'

'The stage.'

'Oh,' I said, not being able to think of anything else to say.

As we passed a large expanse of brick wall he stopped, felt in his pocket and produced a piece of chalk. He ordered me to keep a look-out for anyone who might be walking that way. I went, as ordered, to the other side of the road while he wrote 'Go Home Yanks' and 'Ban Atom Bases' on the wall. We walked on again until he saw another wall upon which he wrote an indecent rhyme beginning, 'Is it true what they say about Eton?' He was so exhausted by the effort of this that for a long while he couldn't speak. Finally he said: 'Don't you get sick of it?'

'Of what?'

'The stage!' he said, eyeing me with ill-concealed contempt.

'No.'

This must have disgusted him more than he showed for when we reached my house he paused before ascending the steps to write on the wall: 'Hang the bleedin' actors.' I snatched his chalk and began to obliterate what he'd written. There was a scuffle, during which I threw the chalk over the fence into the next-door flowerbeds. Bob Kennedy swore, loudly and violently, kicked me on the ankle, and without even bothering to say goodnight, he walked away down the road.

I managed to hobble up the steps into the house. The next morning I had an enormous purple bruise which gave me hell for the next few days.

A shrilling telephone by my bed woke me on Thursday morning. I hadn't had much sleep the night before: a party at Monty Woodward's hadn't finished till two. I heard mother shuffle into the room, lift the receiver and yell: 'Who is it?' After being told she dropped the instrument onto my bed saying 'It's that Sorsby girl again. She's been ringing you for the past two hours.'

'What is it?' I asked Vivian.

'I'm so depressed,' she said. 'Can you meet me?'

'I have a rehearsal at ten-thirty.'

'It – it doesn't matter.'

'I can see you about one, for lunch?'

'OK.' I heard a low moan escape her as she replaced the receiver.

I got up and dressed, had breakfast and arrived at the Rainier Revuebar at ten-twenty. Lottie was in the foyer. She'd taken to hanging around the place even though she no longer worked there. I heard her telling the Countess Sirie what a tedious little quack she thought the new pianist.

'Shouldn't be surprised if he doesn't make a complete hash of your big nude shimmy number, darling,' she was saying as the doors closed upon them.

I slipped upstairs to the dressing room. Outside I met Mr Fitzmaurice looking as though death had taken all his chickens at one fell swoop. I expected at least a nod considering I was dining with him in the evening. Instead of speaking he took me by the hand, led me into the dressing room and pointed to one of the mirrors. It had a large V-shaped crack across it.

'Who's done that?' I said.

'I did.' He looked at me with eyes that would flood with tears at any moment. 'Seven years bad luck, isn't it?'

'Oh really, Mr Fitzmaurice,' I said, 'you don't surely believe those superstitions?'

'No,' he said. I had the feeling he was telling me a fib. 'I'm only worried in case someone is hurt by the glass particles on the floor.'

'Try sellotape – if you stick sellotape over the cracks the mirror will be quite safe. It won't fall out of its frame.'

He rang through to the porter to ask him for a dust-pan. The porter told him that the key to the store cupboard was kept by the cleaner, who was not in the building at present. As I left the room he was still trying to find out if there was a duplicate, which I learned later was not the case.

I went along to the wings to begin my rehearsal. On my way there I passed Lottie bending over a pile of music. She didn't see me. As I sat in the O.P. corner Mr Fitzmaurice slipped into the seat next to mine. How lithe and handsome he was, his hair silvered, his eyes dark with gleams of hidden amusement. There was something about him both vital and rugged and relaxed. When the rehearsal was about to break up, I found him by my side again. 'Look,' he said, in a low voice, 'we haven't decided where you are to meet me tonight.'

'No,' I said.

'How about here – in the foyer. About eight?'

'Yes,' I said.

Ten minutes later I was at a quiet table in the Ali Barber restaurant where I had arranged to meet Vivian Sorsby. She arrived ten minutes late. I had quite a shock upon seeing her. Almost immediately she sat down and burst into tears. I tried to comfort her; it was no use. It appeared that, unexpectedly, she had received a letter inviting her to take a screen test. I began to say that this was no cue for tears, she dabbed a handkerchief to her eyes and motioned for me to be quiet. The test was for the film of Wila S. Gronton's *The Divine Marquisé*. The test had been scheduled for two days previously, and she had read her lines so badly that she was sure she'd never play Pompadour. She'd got the sack from Harrods and the only work she had in hand was to pose for a deodorant advertisement.

'I'm just a failure, Susan,' she said, staring into her soup.

I thought about poor Vivian Sorsby all the way home. She isn't right for Pompadour, I do see that. It does seem unfair, though. Well, I mean – some people get everything and some people get nothing. The world just isn't run on economical lines. If it were, then everyone could count on getting something. I don't often have such deep thoughts and they depressed me slightly. After all – oh it really doesn't matter.

I met Mr Fitzmaurice at eight o'clock in the foyer. At first I couldn't see him for the crush. I had no idea that the Rainier Revuebar was so crowded at night-time. There were a gang of rough looking sailors just going in as I arrived. I didn't like the look of them at all. Mr Fitzmaurice came forward, smiling.

'Miss Hope,' he said, hurrying me out into the street, 'I wonder if you would very much mind – ' Here it comes, I thought, he's going to turn me down. 'If we didn't go to a restaurant?'

'Where do you want to go then?' I said, 'A hot dog stall?'

He gave a jump as though he'd bitten into a bee. 'Why no – Wouldn't you like to come to my place? We could have a meal there?'

'I'd love that,' I said, as he bundled me into a taxi and gave the driver an address in West Hampstead.

We drew up outside a pillared portico – it must have been opulent in 1902, but now the plaster was crumbling, the woodwork badly needed re-painting and the hall smelt of distemper and cats. Inside the main door was a row of bells with names printed under them:

Miss Hillyer-Highet.
J. B. Carlos-Williams.
Mrs Edmund Bowen-Western-Jackson.
Miss Smythe-Foster-Foster.
Miss S.V.M. MacInley (rtrd).
Francis Tagoe (Nigerian Embassy).
The Mahatma Brewster.
Arnold: Confidential Tailoring.

One bell had no name under it and I presumed this belonged to Mr Fitzmaurice.

'What lovely names they all have,' I said, as we mounted the stairs.

Mr Fitzmaurice gave a quiet cough. 'Blacks mostly,' he said, almost running up the second flight.

We paused to allow a man to pass by us carrying a hammered copper kettle, his arms threaded with bracelets. Mr Fitzmaurice nodded affably to him, and we climbed on. The flat occupied by Mr Fitzmaurice was on the top floor, the attics of the original house. The soundproofing wasn't too good, we could hear a party going on – strange music, gongs and cymbals predominating, floated up from the flat below. While Mr Fitz-maurice was in the kitchen fixing a drink I stared from the windows at the street. Every half-second a car went by with a loud whoooof. Suddenly a 'pop' came from the kitchen and closely following this the sound of fizzing, equally closely followed by the appearance of Mr Fitzmaurice wheeling a trolley with food and drink upon it. He was pretty sure I'd agree to come here, I thought.

'Champagne,' he announced in a voice straight from between the covers of *The Sorrows of Satan*.

He handed me a glass, lifted his own, and did his best to smash them both by cracking them together. It must have been the effect of the cymbals below.

'And what do you think of my little place?' He waved the glass about, spilling champagne. 'Not bad, eh? Not at all bad.'

The walls were covered in striped bro-
caded paper, the woodwork was cream, the
furniture Selfridges – perhaps. A table supported a red-fringed lamp which threw a
scarlet glow over Van Gogh's 'Sunflowers',
and cast a dimmer, pinkier radiance across a
Chinese horse. A wooden chandelier hung,
unlit, from the ceiling stretching out four
arms to support four red-fringed shades –
exact replicas in miniature of the one
beneath 'Sunflowers'. We moved on.

'And this is the bedroom, Susan.'

I said: 'Lovely.'

There was a double bed. I noticed that at
once. The room contained little else of
interest.

Mr Fitzmaurice said: 'My kitchen!' with
all the feeling of Cornelia saying 'These are
my jewels.'

I said: 'It's nice.'

'The bathroom!'

'Sort of compact,' I said.

'The loo,' Mr Fitzmaurice said with a
giggle, opening a cream door and shutting it
again rather quickly. 'So if you want to wash
your hands . . . ' He left the rest of the

sentence discreetly to the imagination. 'Now let's get on with our supper.'

Over supper he played French songs to me on the record player, and between us we drank two bottles of cheap champagne. About ten-thirty I began to have trouble walking. I began to titter with a frequency that seemed to alarm Mr Fitzmaurice. Drink usually made me sleepy. I wasn't sleepy now – I felt gay and reckless.

Bunny – we arrived at that stage quite early – said: 'You're a strange girl, Susan.'

I said: 'In what way?' noticing his champagne-stained nylon shirt and the string vest underneath.

He gave a long, world-weary sigh, the kind Ivor Novello, I imagine, might have given – though I never saw him. 'The girls I have to meet, Susan, they're – how shall I put it – well, they have had the bloom rubbed from them.'

I leaned across and re-filled my glass before replying. 'Yes.'

'Yes, they have had to sacrifice the bloom,' he half-muttered, switching out the standard lamp, leaving only the red-fringed one to see by.

All this talk of bloom was getting me confused. 'Let's have another record, Bunny,' I said, doing a hop-skip-and-jump across the room.

'No – do be careful, Susan!' This as I fell heavily upon the floor. 'Do you really want more music?'

'Yes,' I said. Then I had a simply marvellous idea. 'Why don't we play that game where everyone pretends to be someone in history?'

'I'm not good at games.'

'It's quite easy.'

'I'd rather not, Susan.'

'Oh, come on.'

'I'd rather not, if you don't mind.'

'Let yourself go, Bunny.'

I leaned over the back of the studio couch and ruffled his hair. I was totally unprepared for what happened next. About 50 per cent of Mr Fitzmaurice's hair came away in my hand! He leaped to his feet clutching his toupee, and ran for the bathroom mirror. He returning giggling sheepishly.

'Don't say anything to the other girls about this.'

I said: 'I won't breathe a word.'

'I do it for appearance's sake,' he said, giving me a mournful glance, 'I'm not in the least vain.' I couldn't think of any reply. 'The club patrons – they expect it,' Bunny said, after drawing the curtains: 'They expect to see a man looking smart.'

I nodded. He took my hands in his and gazed into my eyes. I thought he was going to ask me if I believed him (which I didn't). Instead of doing what was expected he swiftly fastened himself onto my lips, with something between a snarl and a roar. My knees melted. The champagne, the French songs, the pink lights, and even Bunny's toupee had done their work. I was numb with desire. I struggled, but I was like a bird in his hands. My thoughts whirled round and round, I seemed to be flying through the air, red sparks danced before my eyes. Then, frozen with horror, I realised that Bunny was carrying me in his arms towards the bed-room! I screamed, I struggled, but it was no use. I was so weak and he was so strong. He threw me savagely onto the bed. As I stared up at him, hypnotised like a dove before a hawk, he began to unbutton his shirt. Then I must have fainted. I remember nothing else until Mr Fitzmaurice left me to call a taxi.

I walked after him into the living-room. As I passed the front door of the flat I caught sight of a folded piece of paper, evidently pushed through the door by another tenant. It said:

Dear Fitzmaurice,

I arrived home this evening to find my flat smelling of sulphur. I do not know whether you are in the habit of using this evil-smelling stuff (or for what purpose). If you are conducting any infernal experiments I shall be obliged if you would cease to do so. Owing to the peculiar nature of the conversion any strong odour seeps from your flat into mine. I wish you to appreciate this fact before causing me considerable inconvenience in the future.

Yours faithfully,
Vera MacInley

I refolded the note and gave it to Mr Fitzmaurice. He read it, crumpled it into a ball, threw the ball into the fireplace, retrieved the ball, unfolded it, smoothed it out, read it again, and sat down to write a reply, saying to me as he did so: 'Your taxi will be here in about five minutes, Susan.'

I sat watching him, wondering how a man as respectable as he was could bring himself to take advantage of a girl when she was drunk. A taxi honked loudly in the street. Mr Fitzmaurice put his note in an envelope, addressed it, blotted it and led the way downstairs. He stopped before one of the doors below and pushed the note through the letter-box, a wolfish expression playing about his lips as he did so.

I said goodnight to him, got into the taxi – which he paid for – and resolved to have no qualms about giving in my notice the next day.

The gang came to the first night of *Little by Little*. It was superb! Everyone simply raved about me – though I had only a tiny part, mostly I did Company poses intended to support the Countess Sirie. I had *the* divinest costume for my own special piece. It was a garden and we were all flowers waiting for the Countess Sirie – who was supposed to be a dragon-fly. Just before she entered I did a sort of dance, well I mean – just everybody thought it was sensational. The really amazing scene, of course, was the Countess's. The scene is an elegant chateau overlooking the sea. Sirie is seated at the piano, then she gets up and walks across the stage – just to show the audience that she is fully dressed – she sits down and begins to play. Here, you think, is a superbly accomplished artist. The audience can only see her head as she plays. She seems utterly wrapped in the melody she is playing. Suddenly her hands come down in a thunderous chord, she jumps up – and she is naked! While she has been playing – or pretending to play, the pianist does all the work – she has taken off every stitch of clothing. It really is sensational. So intelligently done. You can literally *feel* intelligence guiding her hand. I had to rush up to her after the applause was over and congratulate her. The Countess Sirie von Blumenghast is a great artist.

I gave my notice in to Mr Fitzmaurice, who was quite surprised when I told him I was going to Mareposa with Lottie. I had the impression that he regretted what he had done to me – he must have clearly seen how he had completely forfeited my respect. I think he was ashamed. I didn't see very much of him before I left London for Liverpool to catch the boat.

I met Lottie at the station. She was travelling with me. She said: 'Thank God, Hope, I thought you were never coming.'

'I'm early,' I said.

She picked up the hold-all she was carrying and began walking towards the platform.

'Keep your eyes peeled for any girl on her own,' she said.

'Why?'

'We're supposed to be meeting Inez Rendlesham.'

I walked behind her for a short space of time, looking round me. I said, finally: 'What does she dress like?'

'I don't know.'

'Then how are we supposed to find her?'

Lottie's eyebrows curled, her lip stiffened, she became tense. 'I don't know,' she said.

'But – '

'Look, Hope, all I can tell you is that I've been told to meet this Rendlesham girl. I haven't a clue what she looks like, but we'll presume she'll dress like a civilised member of society.'

'We have half-an-hour before the train goes, perhaps she hasn't arrived yet.'

Lottie dropped her hold-all in front of an automatic cigarette machine. 'We'll wait here for her,' she said.

We stood looking up and down the platform, straining at each new face that appeared. After twenty-five minutes, when an ominous banging of doors announced the train's imminent departure, a figure appeared strolling down the platform towards us.

Inez Rendlesham was very lovely and austere and intolerant of vulgarity. The first two qualities were obvious to the eye, the third made itself felt in her speech. She wore a loose-fitting coat with dropped shoulders, emphasised by a long dipping collar. Her hair was a rich, gravy brown, and her elegant, tapering hands held a suitcase and an umbrella.

She looked at us as though she had known who we were from the moment she saw us, and said: 'We'd better get onto the train, that ghastly guard is dying to wave his beastly little flag.'

The train was full, Inez climbed into a first-class compartment and opened a box of chocolates. No introductions seemed necessary, Lottie made them just the same.

'This is Miss Hope, Miss Hope meet Miss Rendlesham. I'm Charlotte Phillips.'

The other passengers were reading or smoking, their faces vacant as only faces on trains can be, each lost in his or her own thoughts. A new world was opening for me. The newspaper Lottie had begun to read said: CORPORAL ACCUSED (a fold in the paper) ACTION TO BE TAKEN AGAINST (Lottie's hand blocked my view). I sighed and gazed from the window. Thirty pounds a week! I still couldn't believe it. And in another column of Lottie's paper: STARLINGS EAT BIRDMAN!

The train roared northwards through the fields, green, brown, and cow-covered. The trees rushed past, the streams and bridges ran to meet us and receded. I was on my way.

'Have you been in show-business long?' I asked Inez at the first opportunity.

She showed an eighth of an inch of teeth, and said: 'I'm a straight actress, really.'

'You don't – sing – or anything?'

'Not really.' She shuddered and I thought she was going to be train-sick. It was her way of being amused. 'Ghastly, isn't it?'

'No,' I said, for want of anything better.

Inez said: 'I'm sure you're awfully good – at whatever it is you do.'

'I haven't had many jobs – I got this one through Lot – Charlotte.'

Inez presented me with another view of the bottom of her incisors. 'I'm sure to be too ghastly – what are we supposed to do?' And then she added the fatal word. 'Strip?' An old man with pink National Health frames to his spectacles turned his head in our direction. 'I shan't be any good at that.'

Lottie made a great show of folding her paper. The headline now read: CORP ACCUSED OF ASS. ACT TO BE TAKE. And underneath, 'I had been drinking – '

Lottie said: 'I don't want any kind of trouble from you, Rendlesham, we aren't allowed to show anything. Get that into your head. The authorities in Mareposa don't allow décolletage even. If I hear you mentioning nudity again this trip I'll personally give you the sack and explain to Miss Monteith afterwards.'

Inez looked sourly out of the window. 'I don't see what is so wrong about mentioning it.'

Lottie said: 'It leads to smutty talk. I won't have that. God! These men on board are liable to get the worst ideas anyway. You mention the fact that you're strippers and I'll never get them out of your cabins.'

I said: 'I didn't know there were going to be any men on board.'

'There'll be the crew, stewards and things.'

'I hadn't thought of that,' I said.

'Well don't.' She shivered her nostrils and showed the whites of her eyes. 'I intend to have you enter the Casa de las Conchas without a mark on you,' she said, lowering her voice because the man with National Health frames was listening. 'I shall repeat this to the others but I'll tell you now – ' this in a hoarse whisper ' – if I catch a *man* in anyone's cabin after ten o'clock, whether he's dressed or undressed, I'll send the girl back to England before she can say thank you.'

'What is the Casa de las Conchas?' Inez said, trying to draw the conversation away from dangerous ground.

'The hostel.'

'What's it like?'

'I don't know. Never been there. Miss Monteith says it's pleasant. Think I've a photograph somewhere.'

She dived into her hold-all, produced a handbag, rummaged and found a battered-looking snapshot which she passed to us. It seemed a terribly smart place. The photograph was taken from outside, all one could see was a pair of magnificent wrought iron gates with the name of the house above them. On the left side of the gates stood a statue of a man holding an enormous conch shell in front of him. I was impressed.

Inez glanced at the picture and said: 'What is that ghastly thing he's holding in his hand?'

'A conch shell,' I said.

Lottie said: 'Come on, let's have something to eat. It'll pass the time away.'

Swaying down the corridor we made our way to the dining car. Lottie ordered our meal, we began to eat in silence. It was delicious! – whatever it was, I didn't like to ask.

Inez placed her spoon carefully to one side for future use. 'That old man with the pink frames is watching us,' she all but cackled. 'Let's smile at him – just for the fun of it.'

I wondered if she perhaps weren't deliberately inciting Lottie to violence. Lottie obviously thought this too, she merely paused, a fork half way to her lips, and said: 'Rendlesham! can you think of nothing but *men*?' And the way she pronounced the word carried a lot of meaning.

Inez twitched at the table cloth, almost spilling a glass of water, and shrugged. For the rest of the meal no one spoke, in silence we went back to our compartment. Lottie lit a cigarette, opened the window and began to read something called *A World View of Reverence*. Inez offered me a chocolate. I refused. The train roared on. Once it stopped somewhere and a few people got out and then the rhythm of the wheels began again. Inez yawned.

I said: 'It you can't sing how did you get this job?'

'I was at the Whitehall Academy of Dramatic Art.'

I waited, but this seemed to be the end of the sentence, which apparently should have been self-explanatory.

'How did you get the job, though?' I said.

Inez showed molars, incisors and canines this time and said: 'It was all some ghastly mistake. You see my best friend, Ella – an American student – had spent her return fare to the States. She was utterly desperate because her father is absolutely mingy where money is concerned. There was only one way to get home. She had to get a job in the States which would pay her fare over. Well, this turned up, I mean Mareposa being so near the border, it was perfect.'

She drifted her fingers through the chocolate wrappings to see if she'd missed any.

She said: 'The Registrar at W.A.D.A., an absolute *fool* of a woman called Shrine, confused me with Ella – we were always together, you see. Mrs Shrine came into my class one day, handed me a note and told me to meet a Miss Monteith. So I did. And I got the job. Ella was speechless.'

Finding this amusing she began to laugh, a lock of her rich brown hair came adrift and fell over her face. The wind caught it and blew it back and forth.

I said: 'I wonder how much longer we'll be on this train?'

Nobody bothered to answer me. I stared out of the window. The train shot into a tunnel and I was about to close the window when we emerged from the darkness. The rest of the journey was spent in eating or reading. Inez Rendlesham's conversation was limited, and Lottie had become completely absorbed in her book. Small stations and large stations clashed past. The day wore on. At four-thirty we arrived at Lime Street, struggled stiffly to our feet and got off the train.

'Follow me,' Lottie ordered, threading her way through the crowd.

I had no intention of doing otherwise, but I didn't remark on this. The hotel we were staying at was near the station – too near, I hardly slept for the noise. We pushed into the entrance hall, put our suitcases down and checked in at the desk.

The receptionist raised her skull and opened her eyes: she possessed a face one is unlikely to see anywhere else this side of Jupiter or Mars. Waving her hand in a benign gesture, and laughing, she said, 'Yes?'

Lottie said: 'My name's Phillips. I believe a couple of rooms are reserved.'

The receptionist tried to look as if she were about to say, No, changed her mind and took two keys from the rack behind her.

She said: 'Rooms forty and forty-one. I hope you're comfortable.' We turned to mount the stairs, then she said: 'There is a letter for you, Miss Phillips.'

Lottie took the proffered envelope. We went in search of our rooms.

Later, Lottie said: 'We shall be one short.'

'One short?' I said.

She waved the letter she had received. 'This is from Liz. A girl called Joyce has backed out. We shall be one short.' She snapped a black ready-made bow-tie around her collar, and said: 'If Rendlesham's finished dressing we'll see about some food.'

I said: 'What is going to happen?'

'I'm not sure,' Lottie said (her speech slow, considered, punctuated by thoughtful intervals of silence), 'probably we'll be one short. It doesn't much matter, I should say.'

I suddenly had *the* most simply divine idea. 'Lottie,' I said, 'I have a friend. I'm sure she'd adore to come with us. If there's a vacancy she'd take it like a shot.'

'I suppose it could be managed.'

'I could ring her – she's on the telephone.'

Lottie swung round to reply, very swiftly: 'Alright, Hope, call her up. Ask her if she'll be prepared to come down here at a moment's notice. Get her to stay by the telephone until I call.'

'Lottie!' I said, 'you're an angel.'

'It's nothing to do with me. I have to ask Liz.' She opened the door, almost colliding with Inez.

I dialled the operator, told her Vivian Sorsby's number, then waited. After what seemed like ages I heard Vivian's voice.

'Vivian,' I said, 'listen to me. I have some terribly exciting news.'

'Who is that?'

'Susan Hope.'

'Where are you speaking from?'

'From Liverpool. Listen Vivian, there is a vacancy in the troupe. I've asked Miss Phillips if you could come along – and *darling*, she's quite willing.'

Silence. Utter silence.

I said: 'Vivian! Are you there?'

'Yes,' she said.

'What is the matter?' I could hear her talking to someone.

'I don't want to come all the way to South America,' she said, her voice sounding strange across the wires.

'But – I mean – I thought you wanted a job? You told me you were depressed.'

'That was weeks ago. I'm quite alright now. You'll never guess. I have a job on television. Just a small part and a song.'

I felt numb. I said, 'If you don't want the job I may as well ring off.'

Vivian shrieked, 'No wait a minute,' and began talking to someone in the room with her. She said: 'Thelma's here. She'll take the job, if you like.'

I had a short conversation with Thelma. She promised to go straight home to wait for Lottie's 'phone call. I replaced the receiver feeling damp with perspiration. Inez Rendlesham said: 'What's going on?' I told her. We joined Lottie.

Lottie said: 'Hallo.'

'Have you rung Miss Monteith?' I said.

'Yes. She's out. Sylvie said she'd tell her to ring the moment she came home.'

We had tea. We went for a walk. We had dinner. Miss Monteith rang at nine-thirty. Lottie came back beaming.

'What's your friend's telephone number?' she said.

She fixed everything with Thelma in a matter of minutes. I went to bed feeling so happy. It does make one feel wonderful when something like this comes along, and one can do a good turn for a person one likes.

Thelma arrived the next morning accompanied by the most heavenly man whom she had met on the train. The day crumbled and faded quickly. We were due to go aboard at five o'clock. At twelve we checked out of the hotel and followed Lottie's plodding jungle step on a tour of the city. Black sky, white concrete, a bombed roofless church protected from further damage by rusting barbed wire, names of the fallen on a war-memorial, glossy lavatorial white tiles in the wash-and-brush-up. By the time we reached four o'clock, I had decided that I didn't care for Liverpool. In a tea-shop I said to myself that walking was not my business.

The buses roared and swung in great circles round the city. A siren on the docks hooted and was answered by another. Inez Rendlesham paused for a moment before a shop window filled with sports equipment. We hurried on. A newspaper poster caught my eye: 'Berkeley Square Murder', and another further up the road, 'Duchess Strangled'. Lottie bought a paper. Office workers were coming out of big new buildings, streaming forward thinking of their tea. The crowds began to thicken. Lottie turned up a side street. We reached the docks and she enquired for our ship: the Corona del Mar. I hadn't bothered to ask the name before. Now I realised that it was the one on which Bob Kennedy was sailing.

On the quay I saw a blonde girl detach herself from two others. She had hair like gold-leaf and wore a dress the colour of grass, she shone with vulgarity; she had the glamour of a film-star and the accent of a crow. She greeted Lottie with patronage, peevishness, and amusement – a difficult combination.

'I'm Evelyn Eliot,' she said, putting her hand on Lottie's arm and guiding her to the gangway. 'The other two over there are Delinah Priestley and Edna-May Frost.'

'Thank you for telling me,' Lottie said, drily.

'That's quite alright.'

Edna-May Frost came over and said slowly: 'I should like to be sick.' She looked young and not at all as sure of herself as Evelyn Eliot. Lottie did not listen; she had learnt to be thrifty with her hearing. I cast my mind back over the afternoon feeling glad it was all done with now. I brought my mind back to the present as Lottie led the way up the gangway.

' . . . They tied me on top of the taxi – .' This voice emerged from the gaggle of girls we approached. 'And you'll never guess – he was so worried about hurting me that he whooooooooooooooooooooooooooooop a ship's siren whooooooooooooooooop to tell you the truth I was rather relieved. I hadn't cared for him much. Still – '

'Girls!' Lottie pushed her way into the centre of the group. 'I want you all in my cabin, please. There's a lot to be settled before we sail.'

Evelyn Eliot opened her mouth to speak; what she wanted to say was never heard. Lottie turned and everyone followed her. In the tiny cabin, squashed against its walls we waited while she put on her spectacles.

'Names first,' she said. 'Names, then rules and regulations, then cabins – you'll have to share. Now – ' She unfolded a sheet of paper and began to read, glancing up as each girl answered to her name.

Beryl Muir.
Thelma Griffin.
Susan Hope.
Edna-May Frost.
Inez Rendlesham.
Evelyn Eliot.
Delinah Priestley.
June Wormington.
Janet Raishbrooke.
Joan Fannyjohnson.
And finally, Anne and Paula Pear.

Lottie drew a deep breath, peered about her narrowly, put a cigarette into her mouth and dabbed at her automatic lighter.

'Rules and regulations,' she said.

She hesitated as though something worried her. Something had got to be said which she didn't expect us to understand. 'There are a lot of things that are not nice about the world,' she began. 'Quite a few unpleasant things that can happen to a girl are connected with men.' Her cheeks wobbled. 'On board I want there to be only one sex. Women. That goes for you too, Rendlesham. If I find any girl misbehaving herself I shall take steps to see she doesn't do it again. In bed by ten-thirty. Alone.'

Edna-May Frost said: 'I've never really cared for men myself, Miss Phillips.'

Lottie opened her mouth; cigarette ash fell noiselessly to the ground. 'Good. Smut I absolutely abhor – don't let me catch you talking any. Stay away from the crew. I want to see every girl personally in this cabin tomorrow. I'll let you know what times later. The situation should be quite clear. There's a three-berth cabin, the rest are two-berth.

Hope, Griffin and Rendlesham take the three-berth – you others split how you like. Somebody has to share with me.' She glanced absently around. 'Edna-May, dear, would you mind sharing my cabin?'

Edna-May blushed bright pink with pleasure. 'Oh, no Miss Phillips. Of course not,' she said.

'You're free now. I shan't bother you again today. I'll be stopping by each girl's cabin tonight, just to check.'

On the deck we took a last look at England before we set sail. The sky was bright, the sun was a round orange ball low in the sky, the Mersey slapped brown waves against the side of the ship. Thelma told me what Vivian Sorsby's television job was: she sang a song about a purgative. The sky was darker, the sun was an orange segment, the Mersey slapped brown waves against the side of the ship. All visitors hurried ashore, the gangplank was raised. We set sail. The vast cranes of the shipyards seemed like prehistoric monsters ambling down to the waterhole to drink. The cinemas were beginning their last complete performance, and the taxi ranks were melting and re-forming. In the Rainier Revuebar in Dean Street the Countess Sirie von Blumenghast would be stripping for the third time that evening.

I said goodbye to all that.

Mareposa

Tuesday

It is hot. The coast of Panama, a mile or so distant, glitters fiercely in the sun. We stopped at Colon last night and came through the canal this morning. Tempers are frayed in the heat, though not as much as was anticipated. For over a week now there has been no quarrel – except for the equator incident.

'Isn't it hot?' said Evelyn Eliot, taking off her hat to fan herself. She waited for a reply, receiving none she said, 'Ever since we passed the equator – '

Inez Rendlesham's teeth, which had been sinking into an apple, lifted themselves. She said: 'We haven't passed the equator.'

Evelyn said: 'I think we have, Inez.'

'You're making the most ghastly mistake, darling, the equator is – oh, much further south.'

'We passed the equator – '

'Darling, I don't want to argue but – '

'I asked the purser.'

Inez laughed. 'That was the Tropic of Cancer.' She laughed again. 'The equator, darling, passes through the Belgian Congo, Brazil and Borneo.' She laughed again.

Evelyn Eliot stood up, glanced down at Inez, waved her hand to the purser, and said: 'I'll go and ask him. I won't be long.'

She was gone for an hour. When she returned the incident apparently had been closed. Later I heard her saying to Edna-May Frost, 'Watch out for that Rendlesham woman, she's a jet-propelled bitch.'

'Anyone coming for a stroll?' I said, after Evelyn had gone.

Inez, too busy squeezing sun-tan cream from a tube, didn't answer; Thelma was asleep, Joan Fannyjohnson never spoke unless she was spoken to. I wandered off along the deck. Half-way round the other side I noticed a solitary figure looking at the coast-line. I knew at once who it was.

'Hallo,' I said.

Bob Kennedy said: 'Hallo.'

The sun had turned his face to burnt-gold. He looked terribly handsome: sex personified. I felt a tremendous physical attraction to him. The impact was like a blow. The blood rushed to my cheeks.

He looked at me, and a slow smile formed on his lips. 'What are you doing here?' he said. His eyes burned.

I could feel my blood-pressure rising. My God, Susan, I told myself, what's happening to you? This man has insulted you on every occasion you've been together. What is the *matter*. I managed to get enough breath to say: 'I'm in a troupe, you know.'

'What – dancing?'

'I'm not sure – I think so.' We stood together silently, looking at each other. I wasn't conscious of anyone else on the boat.

'You're not sure. Why did you take the job if you're not sure?'

'You misunderstand me,' I said.

'If you will talk out of your – ' (I flinched at the word he used) 'how can you expect anyone to understand you?'

I walked away. He followed me. 'Would you like to come to my cabin?' he said. I stared at him. 'We could talk about your job there.'

'I'm not allowed to talk to the crew,' I said. I wasn't going to be caught like that.

'You've been talking to me for five minutes.'

'I made a mistake.'

'That's a lovely dress you're wearing,' he said softly.

'It's quite ordinary.'

'It's cut pretty low – you can almost see your navel.'

'I think you're miscast as a sailor,' I said. 'You ought to be writing scripts.'

He pressed me up against the rail. 'I'm off duty for an hour – come to my cabin? I shan't ask you again.'

'I could get the sack for this,' I said, as he closed the door behind us. 'If Lottie found out –'

He said pleasantly, 'She won't find out,' and suddenly seized me and tripped me so that I fell on the floor. I found myself lying on my back; Bob Kennedy, holding me tightly with one hand, was doing his best to disrobe me with the other. I don't know how I found the nerve but in a muffled voice I said, 'In two seconds from now I shall scream so loudly you'll be blown into the Captain's cabin.'

He raised himself until his face was a few inches from mine. He got heavily to his feet and tried to help me sit up. I pushed him away. I managed to get up and sit down on the bunk, dishevelled but quite calm.

'Why did you come here?' He lit a cigarette, threw it away and came over to me.

'I wanted to talk.'

'Talk.' He spat the word past me. 'I'll tell you something about this dancing troupe. I don't believe it's genuine.'

'Of course it is,' I said, not knowing what he was talking about.

'About as genuine as a four pound note.'

I stood up. He came over to me, lifted his hand and brought it across my cheek. I gasped, tears came into my eyes. He seized me by the shoulders and pushed me back onto the bunk. It all seemed a horrible dream. His blond hair reared stiffly from his head, thick blond eyebrows brushed against my nose. His eyes bored into me, watching my every movement like a hunter's gun tracking a bird's flight. I was becoming unnerved, he grabbed me, his voice came hoarsely, 'Scream and you'll get the sack.' I struggled, I heard myself protesting, I couldn't fight him.

I was so worried in case Lottie or any of the girls got to hear of my awful experience. Bob Kennedy pushed me out of his cabin so quickly I didn't have time to straighten my hair. If anyone had seen me I simply would not have known how to explain my appearance. I practically ran to my cabin, praying for it to be empty. It was. After I'd tidied myself I went back to where Thelma was sitting.

'Had a nice walk?' she said.

I said: 'Yes.'

'Rather hot though, wasn't it?'

'It was really.'

'I don't know how you can do it in this heat.' This from Inez Rendlesham who was sun-bathing in something she called a beach-costume. Lottie hadn't seen it yet.

'I don't usually – but something came over me. I felt I just had to.'

I was silent. Inez began to whistle, then

she began to sing 'Look for the Silver Lining'. Then Edna-May sang. Then we all joined, and I found myself singing with them. I remembered something.

'I thought you couldn't sing,' I said to Inez.

Inez made a deprecatory gesture. 'Don't call that ghastly row singing,' she said.

The sun sank lower. We went to tea. The sun set. Inez Rendlesham had to be treated for acute sunburn. In the evening Thelma and I found ourselves alone on deck.

'We arrive tomorrow,' Thelma said.

'Do we?'

'Inez asked the purser.'

The ship had entered the estuary of a river, milky water swirled below us; around the landscape was dark. A faint, eerie susurration, as of trees, could be heard in the distance. A square hand was placed upon my shoulder.

'We'll be dropping anchor at any moment,' Lottie said.

'Tonight?'

'Yes.' Her eyes were wide and sentimental, and in a voice full of emotion she said: 'Well, Griffin and Hope, this is the end of the trip. I want you all to stay on board tonight. No sense in disturbing Señora Josefa at this hour. Tomorrow we'll be saying goodbye.'

I said: 'I'll miss you Lottie.'

Lottie gave a suppressed croak. 'I've thoroughly enjoyed meeting all of you. I don't think there's a bad girl among you. Except for – ' Her eyes became slits as she looked at the water. 'No, I'll be charitable. Well, girls, I want to say goodbye tonight, there'll be no time tomorrow morning.'

'Are you coming with us to the hostel?' I said.

Lottie said: 'No. My job ends with the ship docking at Mareposa. Señora Josefa will send cars for you – I think that's the drill.'

Thelma held out her hand. 'Goodbye Lottie.'

Lottie shuddered with emotion. 'Goodbye Griffin, I hope you'll be happy.'

I said: 'I'm going to promise to write to you, Lottie darling.'

She gripped my hand. 'I don't think you will.' She pulled a man's handkerchief from her pocket and wiped her nose. 'So that's that, girls. Bed by ten-thirty – I'm not relaxing the rules, even if it is your last night.'

She strode away leaving Thelma and I to gaze over the rail. Suddenly we rounded a bend in the river, a rash of electric lights came into view. Mareposa shimmered ahead. Through the air I imagined for a moment that between hoots of the siren I could hear a guitar playing.

We walked on, and the purser, pointing at one great dark cube after another, began to explain to us the geography of the city.

We had arrived.

Thursday

Señora Josefa was heavily made-up in the manner of a Dutch doll, fat, smooth and lifeless except for very beady eyes (doll-like again), so round they gave the impression of being almost completely circular. Which is ridiculous but somehow conveys an idea of her actual appearance. She sat with her handbag upon her knees, driving the car. Two black saloons had arrived to take us from the ship. One was driven by Señora Josefa, the other by an enormous negro chauffeur: so black that the cars seemed to pale beside his skin. The blinds clicked up in the windows of the shops we passed, and the end of the street was lost in a white dust haze; in the cafés men sat sipping drinks and gazing at the people who walked by. 'Isn't it too divine, darlings.' Over the roofs the doves came swooping down to the level of the car windows, a yellow bus swerved to avoid a line of donkeys. 'It's like a film I saw once.'

The beggars were arriving to take their usual place, and all down the wide new road lined with glass-fronted shops selling the latest American cars, through a jungle of ramshackle dwellings which housed the poor, and past white walls, gleaming, sunlit, purple and pink flowers spilling over them, I wondered, as I'd often wondered since, whether Bob Kennedy was in love with me. I hadn't seen him before we left the Corona del Mar. I thought I'd caught a glimpse of him in the street while we were getting into our cars but I was wrong. The men in white suits stared in at us as we stopped, stared after us, disappeared. 'Isn't it hot?' 'This film I saw once – oh well, anyway it's awfully exciting.' I can hardly believe it, I thought, and as the car left the crowds I was homesick for a moment. The Blue Raisin, the Rainier Revuebar, Lottie, Vivian Sorsby and the gang.

The car climbed a hill and allowed a nun to escort a line of children across the road. Turning, my eyes caught a few pepper-trees rattling together, and a concrete cross where a beggar sat. The car followed a long curving

121

road beside the river, and the second car overtook us, tearing ahead, raising clouds of white dust. Inez Rendlesham pointed towards a grey mass further on.

'Is that the Casa de las Conchas?'

Señora Josefa said: 'The Convent of St. Etheldreda.'

Blue flowers, pink, lavender, gold, dust, more dust, yellow buses, donkeys, white walls, white dust, sunlit walls, crosses, doves. The car turned again; a policeman opened the door of the car, grinned, said something to Señora Josefa in Spanish; she replied by poking her finger at him. He stared at us, grinned again and closed the door. We drove between two fountains and a wide stretch of waste ground towards a gate nearly fifteen feet high and, behind a wall, the roofs of a building. 'Here we are,' Señora Josefa said, and we all said nothing for a minute in the car. 'I feel – as if I were going to be sick,' Edna-May said with a touch of gloom.

A newly painted sign hung outside the Casa de las Conches. At the top in white letters it said: HOMBRES, underneath five lines

of Spanish, then MUCHACHOS, and underneath three lines of Spanish. No one could
speak Spanish – Inez Rendlesham said:
'Hombres means men, I think Muchachos
must mean boys.'

Evelyn Eliot stopped tinting her face – 'In
case our producer is there to meet us' – to
say, 'What does the other mean?'

'I don't know.'

Evelyn snapped her compact shut. The
gates slowly opened, pushed by the negro
chauffeur. We drove in, the second car was
there already. The gates slid open to their
fullest extent. The gates closed. We were
surrounded by stone, white walls again,
flowers, a palm tree reared like the neck of a
giraffe up to the roof and beyond. Somewhere a man was singing. 'Dr Gil,' the
chauffeur said by way of explanation, and
waiting for Señora Josefa to come back from
the garage, we heard the thrum thrum of a
guitar which needed tuning. Up on the walls
doves walked to and fro. The man's voice
was droning rhythmically; I caught the
words:

Lulled along the milk-white deeps,
Where the purple baby sleeps,
There the lusty sperm-whale creeps,
In the erotogenic zone.

We sat on the rim of a fountain, it was cool, the flowers on the walls swayed in a sudden puff of hot air, the doves cooed, the scent of cooking drifted from a window, the statue I'd seen in Lottie's photograph – half bathed in shadow – appeared to wink at us.

'This film I saw once – it reminds me of that,' said Joan Fannyjohnson, breaking into a rare burst of speech.

Evelyn Eliot flipped water towards Inez like the temple virgins in *Intolerance*. 'It's like a dream isn't it? What was the film about, Joan?'

Joan stood up, looked towards the gates, gazed up at the walls and said: 'About the white slave trade.'

We sat quite still each one thinking her own thoughts. The doves cooed. The breeze ruffled the water. And I remembered – so many little things.

'Señora Josefa will see you now,' the chauffeur said.

We followed him out of the sunlight across a kind of quadrangle, which reminded me of school and going to see the headmistress. We were guided along an empty passage lined with doors, silent, cool, each one painted a different colour. A faint rustle, as of leaves, could be heard down the passage in which we stood; sometimes, very distantly, the sound of traffic in the city was wafted over those fifteen foot high walls. On the next floor the chauffeur stopped abruptly before a door – a door half-open – he knocked. We entered.

Señora Josefa opened one of the drawers in her desk and told the chauffeur to close the door. Immediately we became silent. On the floor below the guitar-player thrum-thrummed.

Señora Josefa looked up. Our glances met fleetingly.

'I daresay you already know what this place is – ' I sat trembling on the verge of screeching at the top of my voice against the treachery of it all ' – I want to say a few words before we have luncheon. If you make trouble (I hope you won't but *if*) then things can be extremely unpleasant. I do not employ Luis only as a chauffeur. He has other duties.'

The white walls, the glittering white walls, the flowers, the fountain, the man holding a conch, the Casa de las Conchas – I could hardly believe in the betrayal of my trust. Lottie – I swayed, I felt faint. Miss Monteith, Sylvie –

'However,' Señora Josefa said shrugging her shoulders, 'Luis is a nice boy – I hope he will remain nice. I have here a few postcards I would like you to sign. I understand it is a famous English custom always to send cards from where one is staying. I think – ' She gazed from the window for a moment as if deep in thought. 'I think you will say "Having a wonderful time. Will write soon", sign your name at the bottom and address it to your mother.'

Luis presented each of us with an English picture post-card – the kind one buys at Blackpool. Mine showed a woman and a little girl outside a gentlemen's convenience with the caption: 'You'll never be able to follow in your father's footsteps.' Mother would be surprised to receive this from me. Luis's round shining face, his black woolly hair, melancholy mouth and wide, expressionless eyes gave no indication of his thoughts as he collected the post-cards and handed them back to Señora Josefa.

'Now,' she said after she had examined each one carefully, 'we are not yet officially open. The establishment will give a party tomorrow night to which I have invited certain of my good friends in the police force.'

Edna-May gasped. 'The police?'

Thrum, thrum, thrum, went the guitar.

Luis leaned against the door.

Thrum, thrum, thrum, went the guitar.

Señora Josefa said: 'You will be well paid, that is the most important thing. And you need have no fear of anything . . . unexpected happening. You are safer here than in your own homes. Which nowadays is saying little.'

Inez Rendlesham nodded silently without a smile. I wondered what we should do. I realised there was nothing.

Thrum, thrum, thrum, went the guitar.

'Our resident physician Dr Gil de Silóee wishes to visit each girl in her room sometime this evening. I have given him my permission. You will do as you are told.' Her little eyes receded into her head. 'Immediately after luncheon I want to get the vexing problem of a costume settled. You will join me in the wardrobe. Luis will show you the way. Until after luncheon then, young ladies.'

In the dining-room we were silent. Almost green shadows trailed from the palm tree, the interlaced leaves looked dark in contrast to the sky. A clock struck, the warmth oozed in from the patio, no dust, flowers, purple, white, pink, gold, statues, a lichen-covered fountain – it was true. The clock struck again. Inez Rendlesham said: 'What a ghastly thing to happen.'

'Can't we get out – I mean . . . what happened in that film, Joan?' Evelyn Eliot said.

Joan said: 'She was rescued.'

Inez went to the window and stepped outside onto the patio. 'We'd better give up any idea of rescue – those *walls*.'

'Let's go down to the wardrobe,' Joan said.

No one responded; we sat there unable to think of anything, the clock struck again – and Luis, who had entered unseen, suggested it was time to go to the wardrobe. We rose. Luis halted for a moment by a door; a voice could be heard behind it as a faint whisper: 'Twelve. We have room for,' but the last word was lost. In the courtyard Luis pointed. 'That's the wardrobe. If you go through the door. Straight through. You'll find it. Señora Josefa'll be there.'

Down the steps, cool, smelling musty, underground now, no flowers, no dust – the sound of a sewing machine. Señora Josefa came forward to meet us. There was a fierceness in her tread in spite of her bulk, momentarily across the mirrors in the wardrobe she was reflected six times. She flashed a smile to the woman at the sewing machine and said, 'All done?' The woman nodded.

The afternoon seemed endless. As carefully, as exactly as if she were fitting us for a West End play, Señora Josefa took note of our measurements. 'Excellent, Miss

Rendlesham!' She'd give little squeaks of delight and say: 'I've got it,' climb up to a shelf, or disappear into a cupboard to return with a costume over her arm.

'Miss Griffin the Persian Parlour, I think. You will wash your hair tonight, please, Miss Hope and then – have you any black underwear, Miss Rendlesham? Good. I have something here for you. Attractive isn't it?'

Little beady eyes shining, light, quick, fat waddling steps, podgy feet in red shoes, lips parted, clean hands stained with nicotine.

'Boots! Boots – have we any boots? Ah, just the thing. You know how to lace them, Miss Eliot? Excellent. Captain Vasquez for you, and perhaps, though I promise nothing, young José Manuel will visit you. How I shall surprise them both. Oh I am forgetting Miss Priestley.'

The nerves in her neck twitching, pale puffy hands waving, black hair, dyed grey at the temples. She looked at each girl. Eyes beady, shining, red shoes twinkling, lips parted.

'Sisters? How fortunate. Miss Hope, when you have washed your hair tonight come to me. You will be surprised to find how good-looking our policemen are. You imagine them like your Bobbies. Miss Muir is the perfect English rose. I have something very special for her. Dove grey and pearls. Was your father a Spaniard, Miss Rendle-sham? Your mother, then? Why are you called by a Spanish name? Sergeant Jaime will like your red hair, Miss Hope, when you have washed it come to me. Thank you young ladies. Go to your rooms.'

Each room was decorated in a different style. Thelma's looked like the palace of Darius at Persepolis. I felt most at home in the one occupied by Beryl Muir: chintz curtains hung at the windows, a three-piece suite covered in cretonne ranged itself before a tiled fireplace; watercolours and prints were placed upon eye level round the walls. I expected muffins to be on the table. Beryl's costume was so suitable too. Hardly a costume at all. Most of us had to wear too much or not enough. Señora Josefa had dressed me in something which I am not going to mention. She insisted upon my virginal quality and what I wore and the furniture in my room bordered on sacrilege.

I joined Thelma. 'What are we going to do?' I said.

'What can we do?'

I sat upon the couch – lion's claws for legs – and said: 'I feel terribly guilty.'

'Why?'

'If I hadn't called Vivian you wouldn't be here now.'

'You couldn't know.'

'I'm sorry, though.'

Sorry, I thought, as I stared from the window of my small and holy room into the deep green pond of the quadrangle. A few molten eyes of sunlight moved across the stone, and Dr de Silóee went knocking from door to door. Sorry. I walked to the window and back, pausing for a moment to catch myself reflected unawares in the glass, black and white, my mouth unpainted, hands and neck powdered. How could I have known Lottie's treachery, how could I, how? – back to the reflection, a turn on the heel, and again the pale, incredibly virginal face with its moonish stare.

There was a knock on the door. It was cautiously opened and a hand slipped round, then a man slid into the room. Wheels burst under my eyes, the throb, throb, throb of my pulse could have been heard in the next room. A scream writhed up towards my vocal chords. It was Bob Kennedy! I sank onto the bed. I stayed very still, half expecting him to disappear, to hear the doctor's voice assuring me that I would be alright now, except for the hiss of Bob's breath, the faint surgical tinklings of Dr de Silóee, there was silence. Not until he began to walk into the room was there a sound; a click as the door shut.

'You can't stay here,' I said, in a hysterical whisper.

He put his finger to his lips. 'Is there a lock on this door?' I shook my head. 'Who is there to come in?'

'No one,' I said.

He slid a chair under the door-handle and sat down heavily on my bed. 'You're in a hell of a mess,' he said.

'I know,' I said.

'Didn't I tell you it wasn't genuine?'

'Yes.' I sat down beside him. 'How did you get here?'

He said: 'Over the wall.' I stared at him, not able to believe him but unable to think of any other explanation. 'There's a tree. You can't reach it from this side, though.'

Hardly daring to breathe even, we sat upon the bed. Bob had his head on his hands and his eyes on the floor. I thought of the long roads between me and the docks, the white dust, the concrete crosses and the beggars, the dozens of white flower-tinged walls, the cafés, the shops with wide, plate-glass windows full of American cars, the milky waters of the river; slow snakey glid-ings of milky waters carrying a ship to England, to the Blue Raisin, the Rainier Revuebar, to the Countess Sirie stripping behind her piano. I wanted something to happen, I thought, it didn't matter what, I could hate Lottie for this, and looking up I saw the handle of the door turning. Events happened next in swift succession. The floor shuddered as the chair wedged beneath the handle shot across the room. Luis streaked over to Bob Kennedy and in a moment had his arms pinioned. He dragged him to the door shouting loudly for Señora Josefa, who appeared as if by magic at the end of the corridor. The girls crowded from their rooms until she dismissed them with a gesture.

'Luis,' she said, advancing towards us, 'take this young man to number thirteen and lock him in. I think he'll find it difficult to make any trouble from there.' Her eyes shrank as she looked at us. 'I shall be in the wardrobe, Luis, if you should need me.' She half turned, then stopped, looked Bob up and down; going to him she examined his face, hair and body closely. 'I think Don Alvaro de Luna should be *most* interested,' she said, disappearing into the dark.

The night passed slowly – the day quickly. We talked of ways of escape: impossible and possible solutions to the problem. Luis had the keys. There was no known way of obtaining them. I couldn't talk to Bob Kennedy, who remained locked in room thirteen. I thought for a while of loving him; I knew it wouldn't work, he didn't want me – but I had nothing else to do. At seven-thirty Luis knocked on my door and said Señora Josefa would like me to be ready to join the gentlemen by eight. It didn't take long, my costume looked effective at first sight, it was a fake, though – zips in every imaginable place. I joined the others on the balcony and gazed from one to the other of them, from Thelma, a royal nymph with ink-blue eyes, to Inez, carrying her black underwear with remarkable aplomb; Anne and Paula, identical in gym-slips; and Bob Kennedy, wearing a white sailor-suit several sizes too small with a lost look I told myself it would be easy to love. I moved towards them as swiftly as my costume would allow. I felt we ought to pray. A miracle was our only chance.

'What's happening?' I said.

Evelyn cracked her whip, startling the doves from the garden wall. 'A lot of men have arrived, they're waiting for the Chief of Police.'

Inez said: 'Darlings, Spanish men are too sweet, they keep blowing kisses to me. Oh, look –'

Luis had opened the gates to allow a police car to pass through. Señora Josefa appeared in the room behind us, glittering black lace, rouged cheeks, ringed fingers. 'Everyone is eager for the party to begin,' she said. She turned and we followed her down the stairs. A long trestle-table had been placed by the fountain, Señora Josefa handed us each a glass of sherry. I don't remember much of the night – everything seemed confused.

Señora Josefa began a round of lengthy introductions in both Spanish and English:

Captain Vasquez, dark with eyes like green, half-sucked sweets, Captain de Diego de Silóee (the doctor's son), Captains Hipolito, Juan, Ramon, de Peñaflor, Pedro de, Pedro-Luis de, Francisco, Miguel de – and then, the equivalents of P.C.s, José Manuel, seventeen, wearing his cap on the back of his head, Alonso, Pedro, Pedro, Miguel, Felipe, Kusûf, and Pepe-Luis, shy, bold, bald, piggish, indifferent, moustached, square-faced; and Sergeant Jaime, who kissed my hand, and Don Alvaro de Luna, the Chief of Police: a great wave of flesh with red hair and marigold-coloured eyebrows, hooked nose and the manner of an alligator.

Myrtles, arum lilies, the fountain playing, a blue jacaranda tree in full bloom on the other side of the wall, a double row of tamarisks, clipped into the shape of parasols – laughter, meaning glances. Don Alvaro de Luna was bi-lingual, the rest spoke only one language. Inez Rendlesham knew a few Spanish words, mainly the infinitives of verbs and the monosyllable 'si', which she used with devastating effect.

The spicey, drowsy smell of oranges, a pyramid of chicken and red-gold fruit. Tobacco smoke and alcohol. Time passed. The balconies of the house were ornamented with carnation-pinks. The languorous rhythms of the tarantas, a local dance, and of the jota, a song sung around Mareposa. Fluttering of hands, finger-snapping, and clapping of hands with a sharp, dry, clack.

Inez Rendlesham seemed to be telling Captains de Silóee and de Peñaflor the story of her life: 'I'm a straight actress really, you see . . . ' They laughed very loudly, as though they understood the point of what she had said. Evelyn Eliot and Captain Vasquez appeared to be having a fight, refereed by young José Manuel.

Broad shoulders, Señora Josefa – a rose behind her ear now, thrum thrum thrum went the doctor's guitar. Skies indigo, moon a thin white line. Arms akimbo, camellia skins, black eyes and hair, Bob Kennedy's sailor hat full of orange-peel, the soft complexions of the young men were ravishing, the girls, strange, exotic – 'no décolletage allowed in Mareposa'. Treachery, falseness, friendship betrayed. The crackle and fire of castanets was continuous and the strains of music came from every direction. Extraordinary green eyes. Sergeant Jaime, swarthy skinned, but with the general air of a monk. I sat on the edge of the fountain and saw Señora Josefa's be-rouged face and felt a faint nausea. Sergeant Jaime stretched out his hand to touch me. I smiled when all the tension of his muscles could not prevent his hand from trembling.

Under the electric lights the crowd seemed thicker. Señora Josefa, décolleté now showing her wrinkled breast, made a drunken, lunatic speech in Spanish and English calling on us to remember the traditions of . . . I can't remember. Some kind of cue was given and the policemen pursued we screaming girls into the house. In my costume flight was merely a token gesture.

The candles were burning in my room as we entered. The floor creaked. I preceded Sergeant Jaime inside. I was in my small, narrow cell, lit by three candles. The floor was uncarpeted and above the bed, beautifully framed, the same Raphael reproduction that my headmistress kept in her study at school. Oh, I thought, as Sergeant Jaime closed the door softly behind him, and came to me, this isn't the kind of career Miss Parker would have advised.

At daybreak, my face turned to the wall, and before I had seen through the window what tone the light assumed, I knew the kind of day it would be. Skies bruise-blue, cloudless, the sort that in England people gaze at with distrust and say: 'There'll be a storm before tonight.' No sound came from the house or garden. I awoke finally to the knowledge of someone being in the room. Bob Kennedy, a long, heavy piece of wood in his hand, walked towards my bed.

He said: 'We've got to get out of here.' I struggled to sit up. 'Get some clothes on. I've found out where Luis sleeps. If we can catch him before he wakes . . . '

While I dressed (in my own clothes) he explained what he was going to do. How simple he seemed to make it, I thought, putting on my dress as Bob crossed to the door, how simple this is going to be. I picked up my passport. I said: 'I must wake Thelma.'

His eyes fixed themselves on me in an almost maniacal stare. 'You can't,' he whispered, 'you can't risk – '

Something in my look must have told him that it was useless to argue. I said: 'Wait here.' Thelma was sitting, staring out of the window. 'Is anything the matter?' I said.

'No,' Thelma said.

'Get dressed quickly, we haven't much time.'

She did as she was told, automatically, asking no questions. 'Passport?' I said, and she handed it to me. I felt suddenly calm. A bird swooped by the window making a momentary rush of sound, the sky outside was becoming creamy vellum scrawled with pink. Thelma put on her hat, as it she were going to the cinema, gave it a final pat and opened the door. Without turning to see whether we were alone, we began to walk down the corridor between the bright, newly-painted doors to my room. Bob Kennedy was sitting on my bed when we entered. He opened his cigarette-case, but changed his mind and closed it again.

He said: 'Keep out of sight. If anything goes wrong come straight back here.' We nodded. 'Come on, let's get it over with.' He stood up and opened the door. 'We'll soon get out of here.'

I thought of the promise with gratitude but not much hope as we climbed up the stairs, holding our breath against every squeak, to a bedroom at the top. Thelma followed a little behind. The whole house, even the unknown rooms, seemed to be waiting for us. A board creaked somewhere below and a car muttered past the walls. I thought, I wonder what time it is in London? The board creaked again. Waiting on the top stair, I wished it was all over, I wished I knew what was going to happen. The thought of all those unknown rooms waiting was becoming difficult to bear. Bob opened the door slowly and glanced in, then he was gone, the door shut with the faintest click. My mouth was dry, my heart was thudding to itself, pumping blood frantically through my veins. I could hear nothing – I imagined

I heard a groan, only it was too low for a groan, more of a sigh.

One, two, three, four. I counted the seconds. Thelma leant against the banisters and watched the door with a thin flicker of interest. Five, six, seven, eight. She sat on the top stair, her forehead almost touching the wall. Nine, then ten. Eleven. Twelve. I looked from the window, below the fountain was in shadow, it had stopped playing, the water was unruffled by any breeze. Thirteen. Fourteen. And fifteen. I started to whisper something to Thelma, who was sitting with her fists under her chin. I was interrupted in mid-sentence by Bob Kennedy. He said: 'I can't find it.'

He was puzzled and disheartened. We followed him into the bedroom. Luis lay in the bed, his mouth open, the sheets had blood on them: a reddish smear, very noticeable on the white.

'Under the pillow?' I said. Bob shook his head. We searched everywhere, frantically, never knowing which place would be the right one. We were flushed and cross and excited and fearful lest someone might push in through the door and discover us. Suddenly Thelma exclaimed: 'He's got it on him,' and flung the bedclothes back. His key was on a chain around the black neck. Treading extra slowly, we descended the stairs and walked out into the sunlight. We were almost free.

The wrought-iron, already warmed by the sun, shrank back against the wall; the statue watched us, the doves, waking up, cooed a warning to the Señora, the shrill colours of the flowers screamed, as in the fairy-tale the harp screamed, warning the ogre it was being stolen. The road, white and dusty, came to meet us. We were free.

Free? To go where? I said, 'If we could get a lift as far as the border we'd be safe.'

Bob Kennedy's face twisted into a mask of derision; ridicule and mockery spread across his face. He said: 'A lift? Can you speak Spanish? Who do you think would give us a lift?'

I didn't know. I couldn't reply. We walked away down the road, feeling thirsty, feeling frightened, expecting one of Señora Josefa's friendly policemen to stop us at any minute.

The sun rose higher in a thousand splinters of cockerel-coloured light. A car came towards us. I lifted my hand. The car stopped, a man got out, grinned, and spoke six words in English. I felt as if I ought to pray after all. He was going to L.A. We got in the car.

I couldn't keep my eyes off the road. We shall never do it, I thought over and over again. In Castel Pe we saw a policeman walking rapidly down the pavement towards us with his head bent and his hat casting shadows across his face; I held my breath and twisted the fingers of my hands into knots, but he did not see us, people were stepping in his way, he wasn't looking for us. We stopped for a meal. The flies were buzzing round the red and white awning, and an old man kept on saying that they were bigger this year and nobody listened to him.

'How long will it take us to reach L.A.?'

'We'll be there about eight,' Max said.

I said: 'I know somebody who lives there, will it be easy to find him?'

Max said: 'We'll find him.'

Up towards San Juan de los Reyes and on to the border, the miles drummed out at seventy to the hour on the straight, wide, dusty road, the speedometer flickered backwards and forwards, fifty, fifty-five, sixty, seventy, fifty-five, down to the road-house by the new dam at Sanabrias. We had lunch there, and for the second time I nearly told Max everything. But the waitress smiled, brought the menu, brought the bill and somehow I never got a chance, so we went on to L.A. to the hope that I could find Sheldon Hunt, awake, alive, understanding – anything.

After lunch I was tired and wanted to sleep. It occurred to me, half-asleep, watching the sun hop across the baked, thirsty sky (in Santa Cruz we heard a trumpet and drums. An idol was being carried along the narrow streets), that I hardly knew Sheldon. By the road was a dead donkey covered with a crawling, seething blanket of flies which rose into the air as we passed. Cars sometimes followed us for miles and then outpaced us, but the feeling of being followed had left me.

Over the border we plunged up to L.A., roared past San Diego, Max turned by a garage, over a bridge and through a tunnel, along the coast, the surf like white fractures on the water. We stopped for petrol, evening swept the sea, the road, the hoardings, and cast the towns we passed in shadow. L.A. flared ahead. We reached it at eight-ten, Max found us Sheldon's house and, while we were too busy stamping our feet to restore circulation, released the starter and was gone.

Hollywood

Sheldon wasn't in when we arrived. A coloured maid, her eyes starting from her face like snowballs on coal, ushered us into a large, comfortable room to wait for him. Sheldon came home, registered amazement upon seeing me, asked questions, registered disbelief upon receiving answers, registered six different emotions, words for which have not yet been invented, and rang for the maid.

'Where is mother, Petal?' he said.

'Why, Mr Sheldon, she's at a party over at the Lacota Pyrks.'

Sheldon fixed us each a bath and a bed. I wanted nothing more that night.

When Mrs Beowulf A. Hunt arrived down for breakfast early the next afternoon she heard only half of our story before she fainted dead away, and had to be carried back to her room by Hickmott and Hawthorne, the two coloured boys.

Sheldon said: 'You must get some work while you're here. I'll take you over to Theodora – she's too too in Hollywood at the moment where photography is concerned.'

Theodora, who bore a striking resemblance to Oliver Cromwell, had a studio off Ventura Boulevard. Sheldon owned the studio, a good reason why Theodora – who consented to photograph no one un-Oscared – should consent to photograph me. She turned on six spots, turned them off, lowered my neckline, switched out the lights and shone a 250-watt bulb into my eyes, asked Sheldon to leave the room and told me to remove my bra, whipped a towel over (just over) my breasts, took a deep breath, and sprayed water from a syringe over my hair, ordered me to 'hold it' and vanished behind her camera. The proofs, she said, would be ready in a couple of days.

Mrs Hunt was going to a too too party over at Joel Barlow's house in Tower Road and took us along as a kind of peep-show. Mr Barlow arrived in an oversized pea-green machine which I was assured was a car. His wife, Virginia, looking as though she'd been carved from the flesh of a peach, welcomed us, and asked us what we would drink.

I said: 'Anything as long as it's seventy per cent proof.'

She snarled into my face and walked away. Mrs Hunt drew me aside, opened her liver-tinted eyes to their fullest extent (which wasn't nearly as far as most people), and hoarsely informed me of Joel and Virginia's recent recovery from an attack of pancreatitis, a painful ailment caused by too much alcohol.

'You just *mustn't* ask for anything here but fruit juice,' she said, as Mrs Barlow burst into the room like a rocket, holding a highball glass and sniffing at it with a mixture of lust and loathing. 'She was fired from Universal for failing to get over her hang-overs by noon,' was Mrs Hunt's next piece of inside information. 'It made front page news in all the exposé magazines.'

Thelma said: 'I'd like a cigarette.'

Mrs Hunt took a pull at her lime-juice, reached for the large, silver-monogrammed cigarette box on the table beside her and passed it to Thelma, who opened it, glanced inside and handed it back.

'What is the matter?' Mrs Hunt said.

'It's full of anti-nicotine capsules.'

Mrs Hunt looked shocked and asked Mrs Barlow for another 'delicious' mock-highball.

At dinner I sat next to a woman who had attempted suicide when Valentino died and still bore the scars on her wrists. Soft music played in the background. After dinner we watched a new film in silence. The Barlows' Capehart burst into the latest recording of a Bach Cantata. Everyone around me found it excruciatingly lovely. Mrs Hunt dragged me across to a young man with large, rimless glasses who was quietly bitching to himself in the corner.

'This is Cooksey Dibden,' she said, pushing me up against him.

Later she explained that Cooksey was pretty cut up about a letter he had received from Actors Equity warning him that he could be expelled if he appeared drunk on the set again.

'Tell Miss Hope who all these people are, Cooksey.' Mrs Hunt had given an order and now sat back to wait for it to take effect.

Cooksey belched twice, took another pair of glasses from his coat, exchanged them for the ones he was wearing, and said: 'I'm going home.'

Mrs Hunt cracked her teeth at him. 'Over there,' she said to me, 'that woman in the awful dress – she's Enerva Southgate.'

Cooksey came to life. 'Known as old Pomona for the richness of her first fruits,' he said, passing a tongue over his lips.

As the evening progressed I listened to Mrs Hunt and Cooksey Dibden doing a double-bitch act.

'*Life* thought she played with considerable incompetence.'

'That man – no, not *that* one, is – you'll never guess.'

'His present travelling-companion, Phillip somebody or other, calls him Nux Vomica (you wouldn't get that joke, though, Miss Hope).'

Mrs Hunt gave a loud neighing laugh and asked Joel Barlow if he would put her favourite tune on the record-player. A dreary little piece by Brahms thwanged its way through the anti-nicotine pills, and mock-highballs.

'*She* is the biggest blow to culture since the burning of the library at Alexandria,' Mrs Hunt said about an actress I had admired for years.

I went in search of Thelma and Bob Kennedy. I found them sitting on the stairs. So I sat with them, thinking of nothing, and talking of nothing until Mrs Hunt had drunk herself silly on lime-juice and came to take us home.

My proofs come through from Theodora at the end of the week. I didn't care much for her style of photography. Pale, drug-addicted, Ophelia-like, tearful, slutty, streaming with water: the kind of girl Richardson would have let Lovelace deflower in humiliating circumstances. Sheldon took them to Roy Stitson, the agent, he liked them. He did more than like them – he got me a screen test on the strength of them.

When Dahlberg saw the results of my test it set his ulcer back two years. I was given a six-month contract, with option of renewal, at two hundred and fifty dollars a week. In my first film, a re-treated, be-horned *Faust*, I had a minor role: in a vision as Helen, Troy's own Lola-Lola. On the Andromeda lot I met the men in the film. They had names like Kurt, Seth, Shem and Ban, they were simple, uncomplicated, direct, absolutely refreshing, young, brusque, athletic, and could be crude and ungrammatical; they had hard muscled legs, flat bellies, took off their shirts on every occasion to show tanned muscular shoulders, and were all, I was assured by Mrs Hunt, fairies in disguise.

The make-up men went wild about my face. My teeth didn't even have to be capped. They did things to my hair – I still don't know what – and told me not to smile. I sat in a chair for an hour while they gloated upon their find; then I was inspected by Algren Roberts, the cameraman who had just won three awards for his work in *The Gathering Storm*.

Roberts had me turn left and right repeatedly. 'It's a miracle,' he said. 'A miracle.'

During rehearsals of the film I went around with Seth O'Hara, in spite of Mrs Hunt's warning: 'He'll warm the pot alright, Susan, but there isn't going to be any tea.' There wasn't.

Faust had its premier and I started another film – starring this time. The people who notice such things had noticed my voice, legs, face, and personality and put me down as a good investment. My contract was torn up and I was offered another at a thousand dollars a week. I refused, and got one thousand five-hundred.

I never thought of the Casa de las Conches. Six months after we arrived in Los Angeles I heard a plot to overthrow the government had been centred on Mareposa. Bob got a job working for a man who owned an apricot ranch, made money, made more, until he had enough to take us out in his car: first me, then Thelma. He left Hollywood one day, another day he left Los Angeles, and another he left California. I was too tied up with work to notice, or care, I told myself.

Thelma began to go around with Sheldon in his far larger car. Mrs Hunt wasn't too pleased, but she prepared herself for Sheldon's wedding. Thelma surprised everyone by announcing her engagement to a second-rate baseball professional whom she met, married, and divorced, after living in sin with him for a month. At least the record shows that she left him before he was jailed for white-slavery.

My second film, *Heaven Sent*, was the biggest money-spinner since *G.W.T.W.* The sequence where, as the Angel of Death with black wings outspread, I sang the Space-Time-Continuum blues had everyone rushing to buy the L.P. Susan Hope clubs were formed in forty-seven states, ten English cities, three South American republics and I was voted Girl of the Moment from San Francisco to Zanzibar. After that I couldn't go wrong: *The Dance Hostess*, *The Wonderful Miss Brean*, *The Female of the Species*, and *The Gold Digger*, during which I had a nervous breakdown and was suspended.

Helga Jewel, the columnist, had the story across the pages of the magazine she writes for.

Susan Hope, the star of so many movies, is reported to have been suspended from Andromeda for refusing to co-operate with director Penn Warren. Everyone will tell you Miss Hope is a good kid, but what is happening to her these days? Don't look now, Miss Hope, but your career is slipping.

The whole of my suspension, which lasted six months, I spent out of America. I went home.

It was autumn. London was cool, the wind blew the leaves from St James's Park across the Mall and up the steps to the foot of the Wellington column. At six o'clock the sky was bright like Africa, at nine o' clock it was California, and at eleven the clouds began to sail across, and at twelve it was England. The hush and quietness of autumn afternoons in England; blue smoke rose from piles of leaves and weeds in the parks, burning the summer away, letting in winter.

The picture of me arriving in London almost shoved the headlines from the front pages that day. I posed. The flashlight flashed at every step I took. I was interviewed, I was photographed, I went home to bed.

I saw the old gang, only it wasn't the gang any more – not my gang, I knew that. Vivian Sorsby was strange and ill-at-ease with me. She was depressed, she didn't say she had dozens of jobs, she said nothing. I thought she ought to have a purpose in life, so I gave her the address of Jesmond and told her to ring – you never know, I said, you might be lucky. I didn't belong any more. It took me six months to discover this – then I went back to Hollywood.

I arrived back to find a note from Thelma. She had moved in with me while she was awaiting her divorce from Vic – she could cook, which was a help. I had discovered all servants in Hollywood to be either frustrated Bernhardts or homicidal maniacs. The note said:

Have decided to marry Sheldon. We have gone to Rio for the wedding, Mrs Hunt is not too pleased. Don't tell her where we are. Back soon. Love.

The wedding took place in Rio on March 4th, less than twenty-four hours after her divorce from Vic became effective. At that it was none too soon, twin sons were born on August 22nd.

M y suspension came to an end and I was welcomed back to Andromeda with open arms. I tested for *The Divine Marquisé*. My test came through. Dahlberg, they say, died happy: after seeing only half of it he went home and collapsed by the side of his portable altar and was taken to hospital. He died without recognising anyone. I got the part of Pompadour.

Dahlberg Jr. laid his long nose against the frill of a livid green gardenia and said: 'Did any of you callow people see a show called *To Margie with Love*?'

The half-dozen faces soon to be seen on the screen as Louis XV, Catherine, Empress of Russia, Frederick the Great, Voltaire, the Empress Maria-Theresa, and the Marquise de Pompadour, looked blank. Dahlberg Jr. took another sniff at the gardenia.

He said: 'It folded after two nights in '44, we bought the rights, and Dahlberg Sr. liked the music and he thought we could use most of the lyrics . . . anybody not following me?'

I circled the room with my eyes before replying for the others: 'You're going to pinch the music and lyrics of *To Margie with Love* and fit them into *The Divine Marquisé*?'

'Yes,' said Dahlberg Jr.

'Sounds alright to me,' said Louis XV, smoothing his chin with a rasping sound.

'Any difficulties?' I said.

'Not really,' Dahlberg Jr. said, pleased to be asked this question. 'In the original show Margie was in New York where she met Gus, Gus was already married but she didn't let a little thing like that stop her, she became his mistress and went to live in a cottage with him. The second act opens with a visit from two of Margie's old friends, Louella and Bea who tell her she should give up Gus – and so it goes on.'

He laid the gardenia upon the table and waited for somebody to cue him.

'The story fits,' I said, 'What about the lyrics?'

Dahlberg Jr. said: 'We're getting Budd Forester over from New York to tinker with them. Shouldn't be too difficult, it's exactly the same kind of set up.'

'When can I see the script?' I said.

'We'll be through with it in about a week.'

'What are they like – the numbers?'

Dahlberg Jr.'s chest heaved with the irregular fluctuations of his passionate breath. 'We don't anticipate any – unforeseen snags. There were a couple of good raz-a-ma-taz numbers in the original, should do fine for Maria-Theresa and Catherine.' He gave a clever little wink all round. 'Louella and Bea were burlesque queens so their numbers might have been made for this show.'

I still wasn't satisfied. 'What about my numbers?' I said.

He shot about the room for a minute trying to kid everyone he was thinking. I knew his brain was so small a pea would be cramped inside it, so it didn't convince me.

He said: 'Sue, you have five numbers including a dream-sequence which we haven't figured how to alter yet.'

'What do you mean?' I said, in my best occupational manner.

'Well – Margie dreamed she was the best-looking broad at the court of Louis XV,' he said with a 'get out of that one' look.

I said: 'Can't Pompadour dream she's a twentieth-century chorus girl?'

His voice began to speak very rapidly and to grow fainter. He stopped. Lit a cigar and blew out a lot of smoke, frowning at Voltaire. After a suitable pause I asked with extreme tact: 'What's the matter, your clockwork run down?'

He said: 'That was a wonderful idea.'

Catherine the Great, a woman who couldn't say 'yes', rustled her skirt: 'She'll want a credit for it, I expect,' she said in a nasal whine.

There was another pause. Then Dahlberg Jr. said in a voice full of careful wisdom, 'I think I can promise that everything will be taken care of.'

This, to my mind, utterly meaningless remark brought to an end his side of the meeting. He handed us on to Karl Yerby, a man with advanced halitosis who told us nothing we wished to know and adjourned the meeting by saying: 'I'll get in touch with you – ' and was out of the door before he could finish his sentence.

Outside Dahlberg Jr.'s car, complete with chauffeuse, was waiting: all pale oatmeal, to match his own loose-fitting skin. After a lot of facetious chatter he drove away. I went home.

When I got home my maid (I'd been forced to employ one) was showing a gentleman caller to the door. It crossed my mind that callers, gentleman or lady, had ceased to call on me. Ever since I'd told Medusa Vickers, the gossip-columnist, that she was a loud-mouthed harridan with a mind so narrow a needle couldn't be pushed through it, I had noticed a certain coolness from the magazines. *The Hollywood Reporter* carried a neat little item one day, 'Susan Hope's assaulting manner is making her no friends.'

I rang Thelma.

'Well?'

'I've got it.'

'I'm so glad.'

'How's Sheldon?'

'Fine.'

'There are no complications – from mother?'

'No.'

'Dahlberg Jr.'s making a musical of it.'

'I'm so glad.'

'Ring me sometime, when you get back.'

I had a pretty good opinion of myself as a singer, which the box-office receipts didn't contradict. But during those first few days of *The Divine Marquisé* I wondered if I were a hoax. It seemed to me that Madame de Pompadour was just about the lousiest part anybody could have written. I quickly formed the idea that Margie's numbers must have been responsible for her show fading after two nights. Voltaire and Frederick the Great had a number together which, if the Hays Office allowed it, would steal the show. Catherine and Maria-Theresa were well set up, and Louis was an acting part anyway – which just left me.

I fell back, in despair, to acting the songs. I was smart, I growled through Pompadour's numbers, I altered the pace – where the music director would agree. Then I walked out, until Dahlberg Jr. would agree to have at least two new numbers written.

He agreed. I came back.

We started shooting at the end of June. The date is approximate because I cannot remember the exact day. Within the wide, vast, soundproof sound-stage, with its walls tall enough to house an airliner, there was no way of telling whether it were day or night: only by the number of people on the set could one guess. If it was night the place was deserted, if it was day someone would be sure to remark on the fact. Under the girders and cables the arc-lamps poured light down upon the half-dismantled Palace of Versailles, the facade of Notre Dame and the streets of pre-revolution Paris; huge photographic backdrops of the Bassin de Neptune supported by brackets cast long shadows across the stage.

I was called and went to the set, where two anonymous dummies were standing in for Louis and Pompadour. They were having trouble with the lighting. Mailer gave orders to his second in command who yelled them up to the catwalk, high overhead. After an hour of waiting the stand-ins left their position and the stars took over.

A ball was taking place in the Galerie des Glaces at Versailles. Pompadour and Louis had retired to a small alcove – to be alone. The music would be dubbed on later. Silence.

'Silence!' This was from O'Connor, the assistant director. He had a fat, smooth face and a set of primitive-looking teeth. He waved a copy of the script as though it were a conductor's baton. He looked anxiously about him and repeated his order. 'Silence!'

The lights rise, the cameras swing into position, the extras begin to act with a kind of desperation, knowing too well they will be blurred out of focus: a guarantee that nobody obtrudes on the star's scene.

I was standing alone looking into the ballroom. I had quarrelled with Louis, and then he comes to make it up and we sit, with his arms around me, and then we close the curtains of the alcove.

'Cut!'

'Roll 'm.'

'Cut!'

'Roll 'm.'

And again: 'Cut!'

The make-up man hurried forward. I let him dab at my face. O'Connor asked the continuity-girl, a heavy grey-haired twenty-year-old, a question I couldn't hear. She shook her head. O'Connor waved his script, and we began again.

'OK for sound?'

'OK.'

'We're printing this one?'

'Roll 'm.'

And so it goes on. I stared at a reproduction of a portrait of Madame de Pompadour by Francois Boucher, leaning against the Bassin de Neptune. The real Pompadour's face had been painted out and mine substituted. Allowing for the fact that Boucher probably flattered her I think she might have got by in the twentieth century.

'Cut!'

'Look, darlin', when you say "Chérie" don't make it sound like a fruit: it's a "sh" not a "ch". You'll have the front seats peeing themselves if you talk about your cherry.'

Louis XV sucked in his breath. He was a large, muscle-bound oaf who usually played drug peddlers' assistants. He looked pretty silly in his costume and would have looked sillier if he'd worn the wig to match. After seeing him in it, though, they'd decided to cut the period hair-style. Historical accuracy or not, Dahlberg Jr. wasn't having one of his stars appearing on the screen with a French poodle on his head.

Louis said: 'It's a bit of a mouthful – can't we just say "dear"?'

O'Connor went into a scrum with Yerby and finally announced: 'Mr Yerby thinks not. It gives a continental flavour to Louis's character and speech.'

Louis XV muttered a line beneath his breath typical neither of the continent nor the eighteenth century. We broke for lunch.

There was a choice of six places to eat. I could go back to my bungalow on the Andromeda lot. I had food in the ice-box. Or I could go out to one of the five possible places. I went out.

I was parking my car near the '23½' when a woman with a red hat peered impassively through dark glasses at me. I wasn't worried by this; you get all sorts of cranks waiting around the '23½' either to ask for autographs or to shout rude remarks about a star's private life: remarks which are always inaccurate since they have only read them in the exposé magazines. The exposé magazines can never print the truth without exposing themselves. I pushed through the swing-doors and into the large, white-leather, feeding room. Suddenly I was back on the pavement again, staring after the red hat, then I began to run. The red hat wasn't running, she wasn't aware of Hollywood's top singing star tearing along the pavement after her. I caught up with her and walked a few steps behind, wondering if perhaps I'd made a mistake. The woman turned. I hadn't made a mistake.

'Lottie!'

Her nostrils arched like a mare's, she took off her glasses and stared at me. 'Good God, Hope, I never expected to see you here.'

'No,' I said, grimly.

A crowd had begun to gather, at any moment I would see – oh, there she was – Miss Vulture sniffing the wind for prey. 'Why, whatever is the matter, Miss Hope?' Helga Jewel said. She must have left her meal to rush over, her corsage of flowers was littered with crumbs.

'Why nothing, Helga darling. I've just had *the* simply most adorable surprise. This is an old old friend (though not nearly as old as you) and I'm taking her to the "23½" for lunch.'

Helga bared her fangs at me and walked away.

The '23½' had an imposing dining-room and plain cooking, they said. It also had a smaller room upstairs. We had a table to ourselves; I hoped, as sometimes happened, no one would call me across to their larger table. I had a lot of talking to do. The first thing we saw upon entering was a woman in a hat like a blue telephone sitting with an air of frigid composure talking to Helga.

'Who are they?' Lottie said.

I did my piece. 'That (they don't exist apart) is Helga Jewel and Medusa Vickers. They conceal, beneath those outrageous hats, souls which tick like cheap aluminium clocks.' I smiled and waved my hand. Catching my eye, Medusa bowed stiffly, but didn't speak.

'What are you doing here?' I said, as the 'garçon' brought the menu.

Lottie took off her hat. 'Well, Hope, it's a long story.'

I ordered the cheapest thing on the menu. I had grown careful about money. Having had so little, and now having so much, made me count every penny.

Lottie began to eat, relaxing between mouthfuls, to tell me her long story.

She said: 'Liz was pretty furious with the Señora after you and Griffin hopped it. Put up with her for a few months and then – something rather unexpected happened to Rendlesham which meant she would be out of circulation for a bit. Liz wasn't standing any more of it and out she went – the Señora, I mean.'

She crunched loudly on a lettuce leaf. 'Who took over?' I said.

She pursed her lips until they resembled the letter 'O'. I didn't say anything for a moment because I'd realised who took over, and wished to withdraw the question.

Lottie said: 'I took over.'

' 'Bye, 'bye, darling!' a voice shrilly called across the hum of throats swallowing food.

' 'Bye, Helga, 'bye Medi.' A wave of whorish scent teetered by me.

Lottie said: 'I was fed up, nothing to do, I was getting nowhere. Liz offered me the job. Took it like a shot.'

'How are the girls?' I said.

'Very well – Edna-May's with me at the moment, actually.'

'In Hollywood?'

'Yes – well she didn't seem suited and I did need a sort of secretary. I have a lot of figure-work to do. Accounts, oh, I'm busy.'

'What are you doing over here?'

A vague, veiled look dropped across Lottie's face. 'I'm . . . just giving the place the once over.' She shoved her chair back. 'We're getting on nicely now. You heard about the revolution?'

'Yes,' I said.

'God! we could have done with you and Griffin – after the fighting died down. The peons seemed to have cast off more than their chains. My word – '

She stopped in mid-sentence and watched me.

I said: 'When are you going back?'

'I'm here for a couple of days, then I have to be back to meet a new girl from England. We can do with her – '

'Who have you left in charge?'

'Rendlesham.' She said the name with a half mooing cough, and I caught a faint sigh. She said: 'I don't know what I'll do with Rendlesham. She's a problem. I – ' putting on her hat. 'I really think there must be something wrong with her. Dr Gil says not, but – ' She broke off.

'It's been nice seeing you,' I said.

'It has, Hope, hasn't it?'

I intended saying a good deal more than I did. I wanted to reproach her, instead I told her about my film career, about Thelma, and we parted on fairly good terms.

The theatre was dark. I sat between Dahlberg Jr. and O'Connor watching the rushes of the day's shooting. Catherine, Empress of Russia, had just completed a snazzy number called 'Two's a Honeymoon', and was now deep in conversation with a guardsman. The scene ended, Catherine making her exit with a noise an Edwardian Duchess might be expected to make while being undressed by her footman. This mixture of prudery and lecherous abandonment was repeated until the sound was abruptly cut.

Mistily I caught a glimpse of Louis XV disappearing behind a tree.

Dahlberg Jr. turned to face the back of the theatre. 'What's the matter with that projectionist,' he said.

'Hey, for God's sake. You got a marine up there?' This from O'Connor as a burst of cheering unaccompanied by a picture came from the screen.

' . . . Tell me about the Indies, Louis.'

'I pray you, Madam, remember . . . '

'I often think of death when I'm with you.'

Dahlberg groaned, we waited, he lit a cigar, and upon the screen appeared Louis XV in deep conversation with Voltaire.

Louis: 'So? You find this amusing?'

Voltaire: 'Christ, no, your Majesty!'

Louis: 'I do not like being laughed at.'

Voltaire: 'I know that, Louis.'

(He pronounced the king's name in such a peculiar accent it sounded as if he were calling him Lou.)

Around the corner of a pavilion came the inevitable figure of Catherine, Empress of Russia. I was beginning to be sick of the sight of her. I leaned across to Dahlberg Jr. 'I'm going,' I said. He appeared to be asleep, I wasn't sure.

Thelma's living-room had a low glossy black ceiling, two white pillars framed the dining-end. A glass dome in the ceiling focused light on the table. The walls were of Oregon pine boarding – except the one which had a mural of black, blue, green, and red birds pecking each other. The fittings were white, curtains red.

Mrs Hunt said: 'I've just had the most delicious meal,' which was entirely irrelevant to the conversation.

'Where?' I said.

'At the Bug Restaurant.'

'Where's that?'

'Oh – you know.' I didn't, she clearly wasn't going to tell me. I said: 'Is that the one shaped like some kind of a fish?'

'Good heavens, Susan, where do you eat these days?'

I recognised these conversations, we'd had quite a few, they weren't getting anywhere. Mrs Hunt usually ended up by saying she 'couldn't imagine' what I was talking about. Anyway I felt tired.

At the Hollywood preview the audience seemed cool towards *The Divine Marquisé*. Andromeda went mad and spent enormous sums of money advertising it as a rip-roaring chase through the bedrooms of Versailles. The notices were mixed.

A critic no one had ever heard of said: 'I would not be surprised if this film breaks all records.'

Leaving aside the lunatic fringe, *Cue* said: 'Honest to God, what a mess this picture surely is.'

Life thought every actor in the film (except me) played with considerable incompetence. This seemed to be a stock joke where *Life* was concerned, so Dahlberg Jr. didn't worry.

Variety dismissed *The Divine Marquisé* with one word. Dahlberg Jr. sued them.

The critic on *Nightmare*, whose grandfather, Mrs Hunt told me, died in a mental home, thought: 'The splendid era of Louis Quatorze has been vividly re-created,' and

186

'Miss Hope . . . as the lovely and intriguing du Barry . . . simply priceless . . . '

I never forgave that one.

It was shown in London, with a great deal of publicity. Posters in the Underground said it was 'daringly witty', as 'risqué as a dream', as 'unreal as a sunset' and 'frankly stimulating'. The only stimulation I got was when I received my cheque.

The English critics were a mixed bag too.

The Times said I 'played the Marquisé with as much intelligent intensity as the stilted script allowed' but that 'the main distinction comes from Polly-Anne Brooks and Berna Rinehart, thunderously wrecking the thin facade of realism, conniving, chiselling, gin-swigging their respective ways from St. Petersburg and Vienna.'

They won Oscars for the best supports of the year. Supports. I should have had Dahlberg Jr. sack them both.

Whoever it was critting in the *Observer* spelled my name Susanne Hope and said I wasn't as good as Norma Shearer.

A very young critic on an evening paper said: 'What a great artist is Susan Hope!

I have been watching her sing for over a quarter of a century – and she seems to get better with the years. *The Divine Marquisé* is her masterpiece.'

Dahlberg Jr. made tentative enquiries as to whether we could sue him, and found he had plagiarised the passage from an old review of *Mildred Pierce*.

Half the provincial dailies thought the tunes were 'nice', except the ones who said they had a feeling they'd heard them before.

I had a letter from mother who said it was a horrible picture, which besides being an insult to the intelligence of a two-year-old child, was definitely historically inaccurate since Frederick the Great hated Pompadour, Maria-Theresa and Catherine and had statues of them, stark naked, erected on the top of his favourite palace. I wrote back to say that I agreed. After a few weeks mother replied to say she'd seen *The Divine Marquisé* again with 'that Lee-Baxter woman' who had so enjoyed it she wanted to stay in the cinema to await the next performance. She said the film had also misrepresented Voltaire. A woman she knew, who was extremely well-read, had told her something funny about Voltaire – only she couldn't remember what it was.

I wrote by airmail saying, sure there was something funny about Voltaire, and there was something even funnier about the actor who played Voltaire. Mother didn't answer for nearly a year. When she did it was to say that Mrs Lee-Baxter thought I was perfect as Pompadour, but that *she* thought I ought to leave Hollywood while I still had the chance.

I began a new picture, an adaptation of a Broadway musical which I knew would be safe. I began to go out less. I began to drink more. I began to take sleeping pills. I can't trace the exact month or week when my drinking and pill-eating went over the line. I know that one night I took five sodium amytal tablets and the wide red vistas opened up before me.

Somewhere a persistent beating of drums, the beat beat beat of drums, the insistent beat beat beat of drums. The clock in a high tower was striking four o'clock, the road, the white, dusty, endless road, stretching up to the border. Images. The devil in a green sports coat. A hat full of orange-peel, the Bassin de Neptune. The director passed out of sight down the long, white dusty road, and a pink tree-trunk with leaves like fingers uncurling.

How I envy

you young

unmarried men.

The beat beat beat of drums which is the regularity of blood beat beat beating through my veins. The white walls, the statue screaming a warning to the ogre, the envied impudence of a young man who said, who said, the flowers, lavender, gold, white, purple, pink, and the bare empty dining-room at Jesmond, rising up to meet me. Across a sea like blood came a woman floating in a shell who gave me a pear from a bag marked 'Ladies Only'.

How I envy

you young

unmarried men.

Crowds. Noises. Now I was praying, white wigs and borrowed stupidity, illlighted streets, thrum, thrum, thrum of a guitar, the hoot hoot hoot of a ship's siren, the white, dusty, white bare, white white white road and a car streaking to the border.

TRUMPETS.

Drums.

TRUMPETS.

Drums.

a child chasing a ball. the wrought iron gates. a hat full of orange-peel. humming and vibrating, the thrum thrum thrum of, the hoot hoot hoot of, the beat beat beat of, a road, stretching into the distance, into the light, a white white white white road.

I woke up. A bell was buzzing through the house. It was six o'clock in the evening. I stumbled into a dressing-gown and made for the door.

'Hallo,' Bob Kennedy said, as if he'd never been away.

'Hallo,' I said.

We went for a drive in my car, he drove, silent, driving with one hand. He'd grown older and wiser and tougher and more, not less intolerant. So it isn't true that as you grow older – He'd lost his baby-face and I knew he shouldn't be for me, but I was going to say 'yes' when he asked me to marry him. I had the money, he had none. I didn't think that that would bother him. Out of the blue came this particular evening, unexpected, not looked forward to; the wind blowing my hair, pulling the light scarf I wore round my neck out into a long line behind me. I thought of a woman I'd read about who had broken her neck by allowing her scarf to become caught in the wheel of the car she was driving. I took off the scarf.

We stopped the car, it was almost too dark to see, the surf pounded against the shore. I stared into the driving mirror and opened the door. We got out.

We began to laugh at a joke he told me. The sand was still warm from the day's sun, and a sea bird called persistently somewhere along the beach. I lay in his arms, pressed close against him and listened to the smutty, schoolboy jokes; an endless collection picked up from God knows where. Some were funny, some not so funny, and some I thought he'd made up on the spur of the moment. The waves roared below us, the sea bird persistently called, a bat wheeled, like a black lace handkerchief, in front of our faces, then vanished.

'How quiet it is,' I said, but I wasn't thinking of the silence. This is it. I've never wanted anyone like this – ever. It crossed my mind that I'd never wanted anyone, period, except for Seth O'Hara, and I was the wrong shape for him.

'Kiss me,' he said.

I did.

The waves thundered on the beach, the moon sailed into view, the long white lines of surf curled forwards, breaking upon the shore. I felt cold. I sat up and began to make my face up. It was too dark to see myself. I banged the compact shut.

'Marry me,' he said.

I did.

A week later the newspapers announced my engagement. The wedding took place quickly: I didn't want to give the exposé magazines a field day. I needn't have bothered, though. Their editorial conferences were too busy discussing newly-discovered information on the private life of Helga Jewel: information which no decent exposé magazine would lower itself to expose. I was given pearls by the Hunts, diamonds by the studio, a bracelet, said to have once belonged to Catherine of Russia, by an unknown fan, and a baby by Bob Kennedy.

M y son saw *The Divine Marquisé* on television last night. He didn't think much of it. After complaining of its historical inaccuracy and its flagrant violation of probability, he said that his grandmother had told him something funny about Voltaire – only he couldn't remember what it was.